LOTUS

LAND

To Oneata

with great appreciation

William W. Foey

William Wong Foey

LOTUS LAND
Copyright © 2014 by William Wong Foey

ISBN-10: 1937632822
ISBN-13: 978-1-937632-82-3

Library of Congress Control Number: 2014952464

Published by Dark Planet Publishing
www.DarkPlanetPublishing.com

Printed in the United States of America

Cover painting by the author © 2014

Dedicated to my parents

Bill Sr.
M. Susie Foey
And my second mother, Marie White

Contents

The Nam Demon

"Goddamn heat. You'd think this son-of-a-bitch rain would cool things down," quipped a newly arrived soldier.

"Dick head, Nam is Nam, rookie. Get used to it," screeched his sergeant, Bill LaMotta.

The raw recruit cursed his sergeant and his miserable situation under his breath, thinking LaMotta did not notice his retort.

"Kid, shut your fricking mouth. Those slant eyes can hear us even in this monsoon. It's your turn to stand watch. Get to your post. Get your ass in gear," Bill snapped.

The soldier glared at LaMotta for a brief moment before stumbling to his assigned position in the black, wet night.

Bill waited eagerly for the soldier to leave for his night watch. He then pulled a thick marijuana joint from his breast pocket that was wrapped tightly in a plastic bag to keep it dry. As he struggled to light the joint with his favored Zippo lighter, he pondered the value of his life. He was on his third tour in Vietnam. He had grown weary long ago of babysitting pimple-faced kids.

Our third night on patrol and we've yet to see one slant eye, Bill mused in silence. *The son-of-a-bitch LBJ thinks sending me these cherries halfway round the world to shoot gooks is goin' to save the world. It's bullshit,* Bill thought.

There was no campfire to comfort him and his men for fear of detection by the enemy. But the endless boredom and incessant rain made him yearn for just one drag of marijuana smoke. One small flicker of light should do no harm.

Again and again LaMotta clicked his Zippo, but the heavy

downpour prevented him from making even the tiniest spark. Cursing his misery in silent words, he popped the joint into his mouth and began to chew it.

"Shit!" he shouted, no longer caring if the enemy would notice him. Chomping down on the now soggy marijuana, he knew eating it would not provide the high he desired from smoking, but it did create some distraction from the monotony.

Suddenly, he stopped chewing. Even though the night was void of light and the drenching rain was the only discernable noise, he knew from his lengthy time in Nam that someone or something was watching him intensely. Slowly, he raised his M2 rifle, pointing the barrel in the direction of where he thought the entity stood. His mind began to drift. The raindrops pounded his body like tiny pebbles, and it was driving him mad.

LaMotta had killed dozens of the enemy since his arrival in Nam. To be sure, some he had killed in self-defense in the heat of battle, but he had also killed women, children, and even animals while in a state of drunkenness or when high on marijuana. He felt no remorse for his wanton killings, and in fact, made little note of it.

In his native Montana he had bagged hundreds, if not thousands of game animals beginning at age five, when he plinked a sparrow with the BB gun that was given to him by his grandfather for Christmas.

"The slants needed killing. Shooting the four-legged game is just a bit of fun for this country boy," quipped LaMotta as he readied himself to shoot whatever had the nerve to stare at him.

For a second a brilliant flash of lightning lit the landscape. From twenty feet away, LaMotta saw a pair of luminous eyes glaring at him before the black shroud again covered the night. He pondered what he had briefly seen. They were demon eyes, ungodly eyes. Whatever it was, the being's hatred seemed to saturate the air like a heavy mist. LaMotta's thoughts swiftly turned to the safety of the recruit, Jimmy Cartwright, who he had placed on sentry duty. Being hardened by the ugliness of jungle warfare and his own pitiless personality, he cared little for the young men he was in charge of, but nonetheless, he was dedicated to his profession, knowing he was held accountable for the lives of the men in his platoon.

Groping and squinting, he determined his other men, who slept in a circle, were unharmed. In another flash of white light, LaMotta saw a rustling of foliage, but he did not see the recruit who should have been standing guard nearby. Gravely alarmed, LaMotta pulled out his service pistol from inside his vest. Crouching, he crawled on hands and knees to where Cartwright should have stood, as ordered by him.

"Goddamn fricking kid. I'll ram my bayonet up his ass if I find him asleep," cursed LaMotta under his breath.

With his free hand stretched out, he scanned blindly for the kid. Again the night sky lit up with a loud crack of thunder and lightning. Again LaMotta witnessed angry eyes glaring at him through a crease in the dense undergrowth. In an instant, the blackness returned. For the first time since his arrival in Nam, LaMotta felt true fear. Without aiming, he wildly emptied his semi-auto Browning in the vicinity of where he had seen the set of eyes.

His men leaped from a sound sleep in panic. The dozen soldiers joined their sergeant, firing rifles rapidly at an enemy that could not be seen.

Quickly, LaMotta emptied his seven-round pistol, yet continued to pull the trigger in odd belief the gun was still firing.

Hundreds of bullets tore into the dense jungle growth, until finally LaMotta's men had spent all of their rounds.

A soldier politely tapped LaMotta on the shoulder. "Uh, Sarge, I guess whatever was out there is either dead or gone."

For a moment LaMotta stared at the black wall of night, reflecting that the mysterious eyes seemed vaguely familiar.

3

"What did you see, Sarge? V.C.?" asked one of his men.

"Where's Cartwright?" inquired another.

"It was nothing. Cartwright is probably asleep in a hole somewhere," chuckled LaMotta ambiguously. "No gook could survive that many bullets," he quipped to his men, ordering them back to sleep. "It's too dark. We'll look for bodies in the morning."

For the remainder of the night the sergeant stood vigil. The rain had stopped and everything had grown quiet, except for an occasional raindrop pattering on the thick, tropical leaves. LaMotta envisioned the first time he had seen an Asian. His father had taken him and his younger brother, Joe, to Butte for a cattle auction. Bill was only seven at the time, walking hand-in-hand with his father and Joe down the sidewalk of Main Street. Butte was a much smaller town then, with few non-Montana visitors. Approaching from the opposite direction were two young men in their twenties. Bill had never seen such people before. Their eyes were narrow and their skin dark, like the Mexicans he was accustomed to seeing.

"Go back to Jap land. You do not belong here among decent white folks," shouted LaMotta's father as he pushed one, then the other into the gutter and spit on them. "Goddamn Japs. I saw too much of you gooks on the Bataan death march. You slants didn't kill me then, and ya ain't get'n me now."

The two men helped each other off the ground, spoke a few words in their native tongue, bowed to LaMotta's father, then continued walking down the street.

All the while LaMotta's father was cursing, "Bloody, goddamn Japs," when in fact the two men were Chinese immigrants, newly arrived with thoughts of opening the first Chinese restaurant in Butte.

LaMotta's father had always had a penchant for hard liquor, and that night in the hotel room, after consuming nearly a bottle of Jack Daniel's whiskey, he began to

4

hallucinate that his sons were Japanese soldiers who had brutalized him during the great World War II.

LaMotta could not understand at the time why his father was beating him and Joe. It was not the first time his father had beaten them, but it was the first time he had called them "gooks."

"Dad, what is a gook?" whimpered LaMotta as his father struck him and Joe.

His father never answered the question.

LaMotta fought to forget the harsh memories as he sat on a wet stump in the Vietnam jungle. He took out a photo from his wallet of him and his father proudly showing off his first bull elk that he shot the day before his eighteenth birthday, wanting to remember the good times when his father was sober, the days spent hiking in the Bitterroot Range with Dad and Joe.

In the dark he could not see the photo, but he ran his fingers across the surface of the picture he knew by heart. He cackled in silent laughter as to how quickly pleasurable times can turn into tragedy. The day after bagging his trophy elk on his eighteenth birthday, he arose eagerly to the sounds of his mother preparing his favorite breakfast of pancakes topped with a generous helping of strawberries and whipped cream.

As he dressed, he heard the sharp crack of his father's hunting rifle reporting from the barn. Running barefoot, along with his mother and Joe, they rushed to the barn to discover his father's body lying on the ground, the back of his head blown away, bits and pieces of brain matter and skull fragments scattered about the barn walls and floor.

LaMotta's father, Bill Sr., had said nothing to his wife that morning other than he was going to the barn to check on the horses. He had left no note explaining the reason for taking his life. Bill Jr. suspected his father could no longer tolerate the Japanese soldiers he continued to battle in his mind.

There were no tears in his, his mother's, or Joe's eyes. In fact, they felt no outward display of sadness whatsoever. Bill

Jr.'s mother, Julie, ordered the boys to clean up the mess in the barn as if it were some routine ranch chore the brothers did daily.

"Crying and showing off grief is for city folks and people that don't have to work hard. Sons and daughters of Montana have no time for such nonsense," quipped Bill's mother.

LaMotta had mixed emotions toward his father. As with many sons and fathers, it was a love/hate relationship. He wanted to believe his father had loved him, and he wanted to believe his mother loved him, even when she never said a word in protest when Bill Sr. would beat them.

A week following his father's suicide, LaMotta enlisted in the Army. LaMotta recalled his mother wishing him good luck with a tone of indifference when he informed her that he had joined. He would never see or hear from his mother or Joe again.

In the gathering light of dawn steam rose from the damp earth. "Looks like hell, or maybe it is hell," mused LaMotta.

For a moment he thought he saw his mother and brother Joe standing in the mist. He had not seen them in a dozen years. He shouted and waved his hand joyfully. Gradually, LaMotta's mother and brother faded away, staring with vacant, soulless eyes.

"Goddamn Mom, little Joe...we haven't seen each other in over a frickin' decade. Couldn't ya have stayed awhile?" cried LaMotta.

"Who you talkin' to, Sarge?"

A surprised LaMotta spun around to see all his men, who had risen from their sleep, eyeing LaMotta as if their sergeant had gone mad.

"I was chatting with a couple of asshole ghosts," quipped LaMotta.

"Huh?" said one soldier.

"Never mind, you little bastards. No one eats breakfast or heads back to base until we find Cartwright," shrieked LaMotta.

The soldiers spread out in a wide swath, searching for the missing soldier. Tedious hours passed as the soldiers crawled through the dense undergrowth.

"Sarge, Sarge, I found something!" screamed a soldier with a shaky voice.

LaMotta and the others rushed toward the shouts of the soldier. Reaching a small clearing, they saw the recruit crouched down on all fours, puking. Beside him sad a boot belonging to Cartwright.

A soldier picked up the boot, only to quickly drop it. "Holy shit!" he screeched.

LaMotta bent down to examine the boot. At the top of the boot was raw, red flesh. "My God, Cartwright's foot is still in the boot!"

"Where's the rest of the body?" queried one of the men.

LaMotta began to chuckle in a bizarre manner, appearing to be incensed by the horror of the severed foot. "Boys, sorry for laughing, but it reminds me of an old Montana tale where a man-eating Grizzly ate a hunter, leaving only the feet still in the laced-up boots. The paper said 'What a great advertisement for the boot manufacturer—bear-proof boots!'"

LaMotta's men failed to see anything funny about his macabre comment. Some of the men began to throw up, along with the soldier who had found the foot.

"Grab the foot. We'll take it back to base and fill out a report," ordered LaMotta, pointing a finger at one of his men.

Tears began to trickle down one soldier's face.

"Asshole gooks. I want to kill 'em all," screeched one man.

"Ladies, don't forget this frickin' day. The enemy is ruthless. We need to be even more pitiless bad asses than the V.C.," LaMotta exclaimed.

In a show of unity the men shouted, "Cartwright! Cartwright!" joining hands in a circle, not caring if the cries would alert the enemy.

LaMotta felt pleased that he had stirred passion and commitment in his men. He knew it was not likely Cartwright was killed by the V.C. "The gooks get off playing with our minds, but in three tours I've never known a slant to hack off a soldier's foot," reflected LaMotta under his breath.

He wanted his men to hate the enemy to the point that they would enjoy the taking of human life. LaMotta himself had no such qualm about killing life of any sort.

"Mercy will only get ya shipped home in a body bag," stated LaMotta to his men.

The return trek to base was long and laborious as he and his men wrestled through the thick, leech-infested undergrowth. He envisioned the demon eyes that came and went so swiftly he would have missed them had he blinked. LaMotta had seen such eyes somewhere, but where and when were the questions he asked himself repeatedly. He knew whatever it was that he had seen so briefly during the lightning flash hated him and him alone. To cast aside such ominous thoughts, LaMotta's mind drifted to the good memories of the real world. "The real world"—a euphemism American soldiers had for America. He remembered how the mountain trout would be eagerly biting his bait, fattening themselves up to survive the harsh winter ahead, and the melodic sounds of bugling bull elk that he loved hunting so much.

He longed to return to his beloved Montana. But Nam still beckoned to him, not so much out of love of serving his country. Like many Americans soldiers he knew Nam was an unwinnable quagmire and the only reason they hadn't left long ago was because the asshole politicians didn't want America to lose face.

"We can just buy ourselves a new frickn' face," mused LaMotta.

But Nam had its own appeal to him, for all his life he had despised Asians. The yellow slants were the source of all his misery growing up. Why else would his father have beaten him and Joe so frequently? Why else did his father take his own life? Perhaps if he had been a better son he could have saved his father. Hunting and killing the yellow man provided a great feeling of redemption for the shortcomings he surely felt his father had for him.

Returning to base, LaMotta filed his report. *Cause of Cartwright's presumed death unknown.* He then requested a much earned leave to Saigon.

Saigon was the only place in Nam LaMotta felt truly alive. He could lose himself. For most American soldiers the garish capital of South Vietnam was their only solace and escape from their morbid occupation. As a paradox, he enjoyed the company of Vietnamese women, despite his prejudice toward the race. Other than his mother, LaMotta had had no close relationship with any woman, romantically or otherwise, in the real world.

He went to his favorite nightclub, the French Kiss Club, one block off the Dan Bau boulevard. It was one of the few city nightclubs that served genuine Jack Daniel's whiskey.

"You want good time, sailor?" quipped a wide-grinning Vietnamese girl of only sixteen.

LaMotta gulped the nearly full glass of whiskey down in a single swallow, then, holding the glass firmly, slammed it fiercely onto the table, cutting his hand severely. "Bitch, I am a master sergeant in the American Army. I am not some wimp-ass puddle sailor."

Blood pooled and began to drip off the table.

"Be nice soldier, please...you no hurt yourself," said the prostitute as she frantically wrapped a bar towel around LaMotta's wounded hand.

The prostitute poured the whiskey over his wound to cleanse it. The alcohol stung bitterly, but he refused to display any sign of pain. "Damn whore, don't waste good whiskey. It's nothing. Any pain I get in life I deserve," stated LaMotta as he grabbed the woman with his good hand to lead her upstairs to the room where she serviced her customers.

The couple slowly undressed each other, LaMotta's tall, lanky body a sharp contrast to the barely five-foot, stocky prostitute.

"You married, soldier? Have children?" the woman asked, attempting to make small talk.

LaMotta paused before replying, as if uncertain of the answer. "There's no one, you're all whores. I ain't met a bitch yet that didn't demand somethin' from me. I got too close to one of you female slants when I first came to Nam. She claimed I fathered her bastard kid. That was a frickin' joke. She'd seen more pricks than a public urinal. How'd she figure I was the father?" LaMotta shook his head, grinning. "Damn it, I gave the whore three months' worth of my pay. I would have just blown it on Jack Daniel's and whores like you, anyway."

Understanding little English, the prostitute smiled cordially as if to hang on every word her client spoke.

"Silly bitch. She named the bastard Bill," said LaMotta, smiling.

Roughly, LaMotta threw the woman onto the bed, attempting to perform sex with her aggressively. Gazing into the woman's soft brown eyes, they strangely reshaped into the yellow, demon-like eyes he had seen briefly in the jungle. In a cold sweat, LaMotta pushed the woman aside, leaping to his feet and backing up to the bare wall.

"What wrong, soldier man?" asked the prostitute, placing a gentle hand on his shoulder.

LaMotta cried out in pain as if the woman's fingertips burned. He ran naked down the stairs of the nightclub and out into the bustling boulevard. Delirious, LaMotta envisioned he was back in the choking green jungle. Dodging cars, he could not escape the omnipresent demon eyes. In a frantic pursuit, the Saigon police finally caught up with him. Tackling the crazed man, they began to beat him unmercifully. LaMotta lost consciousness.

He came to the following morning, awakened by the

rising tropical sun. His entire body was racked with pain. His skin itched from the heavy blanket that covered his nude body.

As his eyes began to focus, LaMotta saw a tall blond uniformed man sitting beside his bed, grinning and appearing to be amused by LaMotta's plight.

"Captain Sevenson, we have to stop meeting like this. Your wife will be jealous," LaMotta joked.

"Good morning, prick. Lucky for you I have friends on the Saigon police force, which is why you are lying on a bed at the China Beach military hospital, instead of in a Saigon shithole jail. By the way, my condolences, Bill, over losing that Cartwright kid. Don't blame yourself, there ain't no safe place in Nam. I know you do the best you can for your men," quipped LaMotta's immediate commander, Captain Tim Sevenson.

LaMotta shrugged his shoulders apathetically. "I do my frickin' job. They want to keep sending me these zit-faced punks to die. They want me to be their father, mother, and protector. But they expect too much from a drunk Montana redneck," stated LaMotta.

Sevenson smiled wryly, handing LaMotta a flask of fine cognac. LaMotta chugged down the cognac with gusto.

"Quite right, Bill," said Sevenson, after swallowing what was left of the cognac. "They expect too much from all of us."

LaMotta gazed contemptuously at a cheap photo of President Lyndon Johnson, which hung on an otherwise bare wall. "Fuck it. Like cockroaches, too goddamn many slants. Every gook I kill, another thousand are born," spoke LaMotta under his breath.

"Sergeant LaMotta, you have served in this man's Army a dozen years. Go back to Montana and hunt moose or whatever it was that you used to hunt."

LaMotta did not reply immediately, continuing to stare at the photo of his commander-in-chief that adorned the wall.

After a long silence, he turned his eyes to Sevenson, wearing a subtle grin. "Maybe I stay in this frickin' Army 'cause I like killing gooks. Deer and elk are fun to shoot, but that kind of game doesn't shoot back."

Sevenson cackled hysterically, uncertain whether LaMotta's words were sincere or if he was just pulling his chain. As his chuckling subsided, the captain pulled a clipping from the Army's monthly magazine from his coat pocket and handed it to LaMotta.

LaMotta's eyes widened and his mouth tightened, appearing both displeased and surprised.

"Bill, you take a good photo. Tell me, was shooting that mother tiger and her cub as good a sport as shooting one of them Grizzly bears back in the real world?" mused Sevenson.

"Son-of-a-bitch Army photographer, he told me he was just going to use the photo to show off to his girlfriend in the real world how dangerous Nam is. He said nothing 'bout putting it in the Army *Stars and Stripes*."

Sevenson cackled, slapping LaMotta on the back. "Bill, you're now frickin' famous. The great white redneck hunter, Sergeant Bill LaMotta, saves his platoon against a savage man-eating tigress and her equally dangerous cub. Forget the fact that the cub only weighed ten pounds," exclaimed Sevenson, trying to contain his chuckling. "Next to Westermoreland, you're the most famous American soldier in all Nam," he added.

LaMotta wadded the clipping into a ball, tossing it against the wall. "I was bored shitless on patrol last winter in the highlands, not far from where Cartwright bought it."

Sevenson leaned forward, eyeing the soldier who had been under his command for three years. LaMotta had served him well, doing whatever was asked of him, but like so many young men shipped to Nam, their heads were not screwed on straight to begin with, and the grotesqueness of war only tilted their brains even more.

"Bill, I used to shoot quail and deer back home in

Crawford, Texas. We called it sport. But from the looks of your shit-eatin' grin in the photo, you almost peed your pants from shootin' that baby tiger."

Unresponsive, LaMotta grew stone silent, staring at the crumbled news clipping on the floor.

"What's on your mind, Bill?" queried Sevenson.

LaMotta buried his face in his hand. "It was the tiger's mate," he murmured.

"What?" Sevenson asked.

"I killed that son-of-a-bitch's mate and his son." LaMotta shook his head despairingly. "Those frickin' demon eyes I saw the night Cartwright disappeared...it was a male tiger, the mate of the female tiger and the father of the cub I killed. He wants my ass," exclaimed LaMotta.

Sevenson gazed at LaMotta as if the man had gone insane. The captain appeared amused. "How can you be so certain that is what you saw? If it was the tiger, why did he kill Cartwright and not you?"

LaMotta rubbed his bandaged head. Blood trickled down his left temple, but he was too preoccupied to notice the blood or the pain.

"Captain, there is a story I read when I was thirteen in *True Magazine*. The story was about a white hunter hunting Cape buffalo in Africa. After wounding a big buff, the hunter and the guide searched for two days. They would catch glimpses of the bastard's vengeful eyes in the undergrowth, but it would never show enough of himself for a clear shot." LaMotta paused, as if frightened over finishing his story.

"Damn it, Bill, what happened?" Sevenson exclaimed.

"The hunter left empty handed, but returned to Africa a year later with his new bride. The black son-of-a-bitch charged outta nowhere, killing the man's bride instantly. The hunter and his guide tracked the buff for three hours. The asshole bull circled around and charged the poor bastard from the rear. The guide dropped the buff, but not before it satisfied its revenge by killing the hunter with a swift hook from his left horn. Goddamn buff held a grudge for a year, then killed the man's bride first, as sort of an appetizer before the main course."

Sevenson nodded his head in a patronizing manner. "Bill, I see your point. These water buffalo and Nam tigers are more vengeful than my ex-wife," he mused.

"Cape buffalo," LaMotta corrected.

"Water, Cape, whatever. Bill, you're sick and those gook cops beat the shit outta you." Sevenson placed his hand on LaMotta's shoulder like a father concerned for a troubled son. "Forget 'bout the goddamn tiger. He can't hurt you in the real world. Go home, Bill."

LaMotta slapped the captain's hand away. In a quick motion LaMotta snatched the captain's pistol from its holster, shoving the weapon into Sevenson's right hand. With both hands he directed the muzzle toward his chest.

"Captain, kill me now or let me return to the highlands. Like so many soldiers, we ain't fit to live back in the real world."

"Have it your way, Bill," quipped Sevenson.

LaMotta released his grip on the captain's hand. Sevenson placed his pistol back in its holster. Stunned, Sevenson walked to the door, knowing there was little he could do or say to help LaMotta.

"Sarge, you're like a boat adrift in the sea without a sail. Like so many guys under my command whose brains are fried, I can't save your soul. I have enough trouble trying to save myself. Go back to the highlands. Go with God. Goodbye, Bill." The sergeant walked out of the room.

It began to rain intensely, as it often did during the rainy season. LaMotta stood up, standing at attention, and saluted his departing commander. "See ya in hell, Captain," LaMotta chided.

He walked to the high windows and flung them open. Large droplets pelted his naked body. Even though the heavy rain made it impossible to see any discernable objects outside his hospital room, he imagined those demonic eyes of the beast he believed to be the vengeful tiger that taunted him the night Cartwright disappeared. For the first time in his life he felt remorse over the taking of a life...the female tiger and her cub. An odd sense of guilt, considering he had taken a dozen human lives or more, as well as the lives of hundreds of game animals back in Montana.

"The gooks are my enemies. I had every right to kill them. And the elk, deer, and whatever provided food for the table and challenged me. But those tigers weren't much sport. I suppose that makes me an asshole," said LaMotta under his breath.

Closing the windows, he picked the wadded news clipping up off the floor. Gingerly, he unfolded it, trying to smooth out the creases. He thought of Sophie, the whore who claimed he was the father of her son. "Damn yellow whore and my supposed bastard son. What if the kid is my son? Why should I care?" LaMotta said to himself, as he neatly folded the clipping, then placed it in his wallet, which sat on the nightstand.

After two weeks of recuperation, LaMotta felt well enough to return to duty, requesting that he be sent back to the highlands. Other than Sevenson, he had no other visitors. Bribing an aide to smuggle in bottles of Jack Daniel's, he stayed perpetually drunk until the day of his release from the hospital.

At first light, a low ranked private drove LaMotta to the military airport to catch a ride back to the highlands. Countless helicopters came and went like honeybees to their hive. He watched soldiers methodically unload dead soldiers encased in body bags and place them in long rows on the edge of the tarmac. Waiting for his ride, he stood looking skyward, feeling no emotion one way or the other toward the corpses that were only a few paces away from him. When the copter meant to transport LaMotta to the highlands landed, two soldiers aboard greeted him with smiling salutes. LaMotta simply nodded his head rather than return the expected salute, far too engrossed as to what might lie ahead of him upon his return to the highlands.

During his flight he looked down on the intense green jungle canopy, which extended to the horizon, broken by pockets of bare land devoid of any plant or animal life. "Goddamn Agent Orange. They will make the whole frickin' Nam a desert," commented LaMotta on the long journey.

Landing at a makeshift camp in the highlands, newly arrived raw recruits saluted LaMotta as he stepped from the copter. "Son-of-a-bitch zit-faced punks who never fired a gun in their lives, and they expect us to win the war with them," muttered LaMotta under his breath as he half-heartedly returned their salutes.

Storing his gear in the same tent he quartered in before leaving, he noticed a large paw print in the squishy mud in front of his tent. "What the hell is this shit?" he shouted, pointing at the impression.

"Ah, sir, it appears to be the footprint of a cat-like animal," replied a corporal in a shaky voice.

"Idiot! This is a goddamn tiger's paw. Why did the freakin' night sentries not notice a 600-pound or so beast waltzing through camp?" shouted LaMotta, his face only an inch from the corporal's face.

The corporal's eyes danced about, afraid to look LaMotta directly in the eyes. "Sir, I don't know how this animal got into camp undetected," responded the corporal meekly.

LaMotta slapped the side of the man's helmet, causing it to fly off his head. "Stupid prick! You let the men fall asleep on duty. Double the night watch and make damn sure they stay awake," screeched LaMotta as he forcefully gripped the corporal's collar.

"Yes, sir, my apologies, sir," replied the corporal.

LaMotta retreated to his tent, fishing for a bottle of Jack Daniel's in his duffel bag. Finding the bottle, he plopped down on his cot, tossing the bottle cap on the floor. He lay down, gulping the liquor down in hard swallows. "Why didn't the tiger attack any of my men?" LaMotta asked himself. He grinned wryly, already knowing the answer to his question. "The male tiger came looking for me. He didn't care about the others in the camp, he wanted me. Screw you," LaMotta said under his breath as he emptied the bottle.

In the morning, LaMotta hiked from camp with seven men under his command for a seven-day reconnaissance mission. Their main goal was to locate enemy activity and call in air strikes. They were not far from the Ho Chi Minh Trail complex where North Vietnamese military moved undetected, zigzagging through Laos and Cambodia, then into South Vietnam. They spent monotonous hours traipsing through the humid jungle undergrowth, being mocked by monkeys overhead, pricked by tree branches covered with thorns, and stung by insects that constantly swarmed around their heads.

On the morning of the fifth day they stumbled upon an unnamed village, one of the many that dotted the highlands. Encircling the village, LaMotta, in broken Vietnamese, ordered the villagers to exit their huts for questioning and inspection. The hundred-some villagers, mostly women, children, and the elderly, stood silently in line in the open center of the village. Some of the soldiers searched the primitive clay huts methodically for anything that would indicate they aided the enemy. Other soldiers pointed their rifles in a menacing manner at the assembled villagers as LaMotta strutted slowly past each individual, glaring directly into their eyes, looking for the slightest hint of anxiousness that might signal they were collaborating with the North Vietnamese. In what little of the native language he understood, he would ask each one of them if they were friends of the Vietcong. They would respond in broken English, "No V.C., no V.C."

Trusting none of them, he shook small children and old

women, at times pushing them to the ground, only to hear the reply, "No V.C."

LaMotta, growing increasingly frustrated, turned to the third row of villagers. He stopped abruptly, his mouth dropping in shock. "Sophie?" said LaMotta under his breath, recognizing the first prostitute he'd had a liaison with upon his arrival in Nam. The thirty-year-old woman smiled warmly as she held LaMotta's alleged son.

Her appearance was a sharp contrast to her appearance in her working days in Saigon. She wore no makeup, and instead of the glossy silk Chinese dresses with the split sides, she now dressed in drab present clothing.

"What are you doing in this shithole?" asked LaMotta.

Sophie held the bundled infant out, hoping LaMotta would hold the child. LaMotta refused, and brushed the boy aside.

"Saigon no good. I come home to raise your son in better place. Saigon no good," responded Sophie. "Billy, please, you hold Bill Jr."

Reluctantly, LaMotta held the baby. The infant looked up toward him, appearing contented, as if to acknowledge the meeting of his father for the first time. With close scrutiny, LaMotta studied the baby's features, whose gray eyes matched his own. For a moment LaMotta showed in his face a bond with the child.

"He your son, Bill," said Sophie with pride.

"Sarge, he does have your eyes," interjected one soldier, lowering his rifle to admire the boy.

LaMotta shoved the infant back into the mother's arms. "Goddamn ya, soldier, do your job," commanded LaMotta, slapping the soldier's helmet.

"Yes, sir," stammered the soldier obsequiously as he aimed his rifle toward the villagers.

Startled by LaMotta's shouting, the child began to cry. Rocking the boy gently, Sophie began speaking softly in Vietnamese. "Billy, he your son. You take America, please," pleaded Sophie.

Deep inside him, he knew the child was his, but he found it difficult to show any outward affection toward anyone. "Ya deep yella bitch, sell your bastard to some other American soldier who will believe your bullshit."

LaMotta continued his inspection of the villagers. Incessantly, Sophie shadowed him, pleading for her baby's welfare. With growing annoyance, LaMotta shoved Sophie and her baby, causing them to fall onto the muddy earth. An elderly man with a stooped back assisted Sophie and the baby off the ground. He cleaned their smudged faces with his sleeve, then the man made funny faces, calming the child. Showing no concern, LaMotta went on to the next villager in line, asking a young boy if any V.C. had recently visited the village. Before the boy could answer, an excited soldier ran from one of the huts.

"Sergeant, come quick! Check this out," shouted the soldier, pointing a finger at the hut.

Stepping quickly, LaMotta entered the hut. Inside was a shallow pit that had been covered with straw mats and boards. The pit contained dozens of rifles, explosives, and ammunition. In heated anger, LaMotta stormed out of the hut, asking in Vietnamese who lived there.

Defiantly, the villagers looked straight ahead, refusing to speak.

"Goddamn smart-ass gooks, ya think you can shit on me?" LaMotta took a firm grip on the wrist of the old man who had aided Sophie and her child. Dragging him front and center, he threw the man to the ground. Swiftly he drew a pistol from his shoulder holster and pressed the muzzle against the man's left temple. LaMotta asked once more in Vietnamese who lived in the hut and stored the cache of weapons. The man appeared quite willing to die rather than answer LaMotta's persistent questions.

LaMotta began to perspire heavily. His gun hand trembled uncontrollably. "Answer me, you slant-eyed son-of-a-bitch." LaMotta tried to pull the trigger, but could not. He'd had a deep-seated prejudice toward any non-white his entire life, but he could not help but feel a grudging respect for the elderly man, who would rather die than be a traitor to his convictions.

A tanned woman's hand covered the muzzle of LaMotta's pistol. "Billy, you no kill, he my father. Hut belong to me," said Sophie.

LaMotta released a breath of air in frustration. "Sophie, I don't know what to say. You shame your people of the South," he said, showing a look of disappointment.

"I no ask American come to Nam, you shame me," responded Sophie.

Perplexed, he rolled his eyes, sitting oddly on a stump while his men and villagers stood in equal confusion, waiting for LaMotta's decision regarding the village's fate.

"Burn the village. I'll call for choppers to take the villagers to a detention camp outside of Saigon."

Some of the villagers who understood a little English translated to the others LaMotta's harsh decision. Some of the natives dropped to their knees, sobbing, while many others rushed to the soldiers, pleading with them to not burn their homes. A few zealous soldiers savagely struck villagers over their heads with their rifle butts.

"Kill 'em all, then we can go back to the real world," spoke one soldier, chuckling as he watched the flames grow higher from a hut he had just set fire to.

Soon the entire village was engulfed in flames. The heat and the choking smoke was becoming unbearable for everyone. The natives huddled around the common well. The few young males in the village and the young women hurriedly pulled up buckets of well water, dousing the old and the children.

During the chaotic scene, a muffled cry went unnoticed, drowned out by the loud sobbing and words of protest from the villagers.

"Where's Bernie?" asked LaMotta as he oversaw the razing of the village.

His men shrugged their shoulders, unaware that the man had disappeared until LaMotta made note of it. In the constantly shifting smoke, another cry rang out from another soldier, who became obscured by the heavy smoke.

"Shit, Woods is gone, Sarge," shouted a soldier, who had been standing by the missing man only a second or two before.

LaMotta ordered his men to quickly form a small, tight circle in anticipation of an enemy attack.

Sophie's father began to cackle with amusement, mumbling in his native tongue.

"Sophie, what is the ol' fool saying?" LaMotta inquired.

"Father say the Nam Demon come for revenge of American rape of South Vietnam."

LaMotta smiled wryly. "Are you talking about that goddamn cat? It's not the enemy out there, at least not the two-legged kind."

"Billy, it is Nam Demon, he is devil in soul of tiger," said Sophie.

LaMotta cackled even louder. "It don't make no difference, demon, devil, tiger. His revenge is personal. He comes for me. I killed his frickin' mate and son."

Sophie stared at him in shock. "Billy, you kill demon's mate and child, you make bad karma. He kill me and Billy Jr. You no good man, Billy. Why you kill mamma and baby?"

LaMotta suddenly directed his attention away from Sophie. "Sophie, I kill things for the fun of it. I will not let that demon eat you and Billy Jr., I promise."

His eyes scanned the surrounding jungle. Like the night Cartwright disappeared, he sensed something hateful was observing him and his men.

"Sarge, shouldn't we send out a search party for Bernie and Woods?" whispered a corporal.

"Dumb-ass, we all take the same risks working in this

shithole, I can't spare..."

A loud burst of automatic gunfire from several weapons prevented LaMotta from completing his sentence.

"Stop! Stop, you idiots. What the freak are you dickheads shootin' at?" LaMotta screeched.

"There, Sarge. There, I saw it. The leaves, they moved," exclaimed the soldier who had fired first.

LaMotta directed two of his men to inspect the spot they had fired upon. Cautiously, the two men stepped into the thick undergrowth, the vegetation so dense they had to crawl in some places. A loud gasp of horror rang out from the blanket of green foliage. Swiftly, the two men scurried back out into the open as if being pursued by an invisible attacker.

Their faces were ashen. Their bodies shook uncontrollably as they struggled to speak.

"Goddamn it, man, speak up," commanded LaMotta.

"Sarge, they're dead, Woods and Bernie are..." mumbled one of the soldiers, unable to finish the sentence.

An agitated LaMotta grasped the soldier's collar and pulled his face close. "Ya damn pussies. Both of you men have seen casualties before," he shouted.

The two men tried to get a hold of themselves. The corporal handed them his water canteen. After a long swallow, one of the soldiers wiped the dripping perspiration from his face.

"Sarge, both Bernie's and Woods's heads are missing. It's as if whoever or whatever did them in wanted a trophy souvenir."

LaMotta shook his head in disgust. He asked for volunteers to fetch the bodies, promising each a bottle of Jack Daniel's on their next rotation to Saigon. The villagers watched in horror as the soldiers dragged the bodies onto the village square, many saying "the Nam Demon" in their native tongue as they dropped to their knees in prayer.

Sophie's father spoke to LaMotta in his language with a small, wry smile.

22

"What's your papa saying to me now?" LaMotta asked Sophie.

"He say the Nam Demon is an evil spirit that cannot die. He will soon have your head."

LaMotta's eyes burned with insult. "Tell your father to go to hell. I will have that fricking tiger's head mounted alongside my trophy buck I left back in Montana."

Sophie translated LaMotta's words to her father. Her father cackled mockingly. No longer able to contain his anger and frustration, LaMotta drew his pistol from his holster, slamming back the action to chamber a round, pointing it at Sophie's father.

"No damn gook will laugh at me," shouted LaMotta.

Sophie quickly placed herself between her father and LaMotta. "Billy, you no kill father. Kill me, my life no value," exclaimed Sophie.

Intervening, the corporal placed his thumb between the cocked hammer and the firing pin.

"Sarge, we have to get our asses in gear now. The V.C. will surely notice all the flames and smoke. They'll be on our asses before ya know it," he said as he pulled LaMotta's pistol from his hand and placed the weapon back in the holster.

LaMotta was so overcome with emotion he could only utter the words, "Corporal, move the gooks out."

The trek to the soldiers' base camp was arduous and dangerous. The children and infants who were too small and unsuited for the long walk were carried on the backs of the soldiers.

Arriving at the camp at sundown, the villagers fell to the ground, exhausted and pleading for water. Sophie ran to LaMotta, tugging at his arm, begging for water for their child and the others.

"I have scarcely enough drinking water for my men," retorted LaMotta. "Give water to Sophie and her bastard," he ordered as an afterthought.

Ignoring LaMotta's orders to give water only to Sophie

and her baby, the corporal and the other soldiers gave what water they had to all the villagers.

LaMotta radioed for large CH-46 transport choppers to come in the morning to take the villagers to the detention camp and retrieve the two dead soldiers. Retiring to his tent, he quickly stripped to the waist for a bit of relief from the oppressive heat. Sitting on his cot, he removed a bottle of Jack Daniel's he had hidden under the pillow.

LaMotta felt consumed by the possibility that he was the father of Sophie's child. He'd found it difficult to feel any closeness to anyone throughout his life. Even with his parents and brother there had always been a certain distance.

He chuckled, contemplating how odd a pair they would look teaching a half-yellow boy to deer hunt back in Montana. His father had taught him to hate the slant eyes, or anyone not white, for that matter. He smiled in reflection, remembering the time he was twelve when he threw a chink kid into the garbage dumpster. The chink kid had just recently moved into the neighborhood with his family. LaMotta's father had hugged and praised him for giving the kid such a warm reception. It was one of the few times his dad had said a kind word to him.

Growing crazed by his circumstances and the whiskey, he began to cackle insanely. LaMotta could no longer rationalize or even understand his hatred or reason for killing the yellows.

A soft tapping of the tent flap drew LaMotta from his thoughts. "Who the hell is it? What da ya want?" he shouted.

"My apologies, Sarge. Your lady friend ran to your tent before I could grab her," said the corporal as he held Sophie's forearm firmly.

LaMotta slapped on his shirt and shoved his whiskey bottle under the pillow. "Goddamn it, corporal, this bitch is not my girlfriend, but I'll speak to her. Leave us alone," he exclaimed. "Sit," he ordered Sophie, pointing to a canvas folding chair.

Timidly, Sophie sat down, showing obvious nervousness.

"Billy, I no traitor. Father, he no tell me guns buried in my hut." She dropped to her knees, sobbing heavily. She held on to LaMotta's knees, squeezing his pants legs tightly as if dangling from a high cliff, clinging for her life.

"Take me and son to America. I make you happy," said Sophie in a pleading voice.

LaMotta chuckled at the woman's begging. "You and your bastard want to live in the real world, what the chinks call America, Gim Sam, or the Gold Mountain? What is the fascination with America?"

LaMotta stood up while Sophie remained on her knees, her arms wrapped tightly around his legs. He gazed downward at her with a smug look, amused by the woman's hysteria.

"I no traitor. You no take me and Billy to America, the evil spirit cannot die. He kill us, then ghosts of his woman and son you kill haunt us in next life," Sophie exclaimed.

"I'll show you whether that evil spirit can die," chided LaMotta as he lifted his pistol from the nightstand, cocked it, and fired a round upwards, putting a small circular hole in the tent ceiling.

Sophie covered her ears in alarm. Several soldiers stormed the tent, brandishing their rifles. Cackling madly, LaMotta dismissed his men, explaining to them his gun had gone off accidentally.

"Billy, you crazy man," quipped Sophie.

LaMotta tossed the pistol onto the floor as he plunked down on the cot, burying his face in his hands. Trying to clear his mind, he realized Sophie's needs were nothing to laugh at. He thought of his own wasted life. Why was he afraid of commitment? He had never had a girlfriend or a wife, he had never had sex with a woman that he didn't have to pay for. With a thin face and bug eyes, women didn't find him very attractive.

"But then, a lot of ugly men found wives and had

children," he mused while staring at the frightened woman who sat on the tent floor crying. He felt something for Sophie. Whether it was genuine love, he was not sure. *Having a wife and child and growing old together is what normal men do, don't they?* he thought. He thought of the day his father took his own life. His father was not happy, even with a wife and two sons.

LaMotta opened the tent flap and called for the corporal. "Corporal, escort this lady back to the other gooks."

Sophie refused to leave, causing the corporal to drag her by her arms. "Billy, please, you take son America. He not know pain. He not know lonely in America," she cried as her limp body was pulled away.

"Woman, you're a slant-eyed whore. I bedded you out of boredom because I was tired of using my hand," retorted LaMotta, unwilling to look her in the eyes. "You can feel pain and loneliness anywhere, not just in fricking Nam," he spoke under his breath.

A loud shriek pierced the black night, like the cries of a mad woman, but with the tone of something not human. Many of the villagers spoke in fear that it was the cry of the Nam Demon. The soldiers stood vigilantly, ready for an attack of whatever, be it man or beast.

For the remainder of the night the cries continued. Although both villagers and soldiers were fatigued, they remained awake, waiting for the assault that never came. Gradually, the dark shroud of night faded to a pale pink as a blood-red sun ascended over the highlands.

As with water, LaMotta ordered the soldiers to only give rations to Sophie and her infant. Again disobeying orders, the soldiers distributed all of their rations to the hungry villagers, leaving none for themselves.

Frowning at his men's disobedience, LaMotta chose to say nothing, thinking that if his men wanted to give away their breakfast, that was their privilege. Shrugging, he drank his breakfast of cherished whiskey.

LaMotta walked to where the two headless bodies of Woods and Bernie had been placed. Though wrapped tightly in canvas, flies already covered the blood-soaked tarps.

"Son-of-a-bitch devil cat, ya took three of my men. How ya think that's goin' to look on my record?" LaMotta said under his breath. He knew the tiger had a right to hate him and deserved retribution. He had taken the tiger's mate and cub without good cause or fair chase. "I can't undo the harm I caused, but that big cat will probably get himself another mate," LaMotta reasoned. "Perhaps it is time to go back to the real world. I owe the cat a debt which I cannot repay...but my debt to Sophie and her bastard can be repaid," LaMotta said to himself.

Standing over the corpses, LaMotta bowed his head. Though never a religious man, he spoke a silent prayer for the well-being of the three dead soldiers, asking their forgiveness. He had seen countless American soldiers die since his arrival in Nam, but never as a result of his own callous act. He turned his attention to the rugged hills, reflecting on Nam's great natural beauty. Were it not for the damn war, he would have enjoyed hiking the wild land, hunting and fishing.

"Fricking Nam Demon. Sorry to disappoint you, but I'm going back to the real world. Ya can have my ass some other goddamn time," LaMotta spoke, as if the tiger stood before him.

A small child tugged at LaMotta's pants leg, speaking in his mountain language and asking where he and his family were being taken. Not understanding or caring, LaMotta directed the boy's mother to look after him. Watching the mother lead her child back to the village group, he saw Sophie breastfeeding her son. He pondered how American-Asian kids were treated like shit in Nam. "Like the way I treated yellows my whole life," he chuckled.

With hesitant steps he approached Sophie and the child. Like every one of her people, her face looked pained and anxious over an uncertain future. Speaking in his usual, direct voice, LaMotta began to stutter nervously.

"I...I...uh...Soph...you win. I will take you and your son...uh, our son, to America."

Stunned, Sophie struggled to stand up. LaMotta took hold of her free hand, pulling her and the infant up. He wanted to embrace them, but being a private man, it was easier for him to face physical danger than bare his soul to anyone. His eyes averted from hers. She stood on her tiptoes and kissed him on the cheek.

"Billy, I be good wife. I make no trouble. Son be no worry."

LaMotta merely nodded his head slightly, his eyes still averted from hers, hoping he had made the right decision. He stood awkwardly, not knowing what other words to say. As he did, the sound of whirling chopper blades could be heard in the distance.

"We'll be standing atop the Gold Mountain before you know it," quipped LaMotta, smiling, finally thinking of something appropriate to say before they boarded the choppers.

Acting swiftly, he ordered his men to prepare loading the villagers onto the choppers. Forming orderly lines, the villagers watched in awe as the enormous CH-46 helicopters approached. The villagers clung to each other tightly in the strong down-thrust as the choppers landed. Painted entirely black, the aircraft gave the appearance of malevolent floating whales. LaMotta held back, making certain everyone boarded safely. Sophie stood last in line with her infant, waiting to board with LaMotta.

The noise of the chopper turbines was deafening as LaMotta assisted the elderly and small children aboard one of the three aircraft. As everyone boarded, LaMotta saw a soldier look in horror at something outside. Verbal communication being impossible, he desperately motioned to LaMotta to look behind him. LaMotta turned, and in disbelief saw the avenging tiger sprinting toward Sophie and her infant, who stood no more than ten paces away from LaMotta. Though the cat's attack was occurring almost in the blink of an eye, everything seemed to unfold in slow motion. LaMotta watched helplessly as the tiger pulled Sophie down as easily as a rag doll. Her baby skidded several feet away from her as her body slammed against the earth. Sophie's father stood frozen in shock.

LaMotta aimed his pistol at the tiger, but was afraid to shoot for fear of hitting Sophie or the child. The vengeful beast's eyes glowed like hot embers as he ripped at Sophie's throat, tearing out her windpipe and jugular, killing her instantly.

Witnessing her death, LaMotta fired his pistol rapidly in a blind rage. Although the tiger was at close range, none of the bullets hit their intended target. The tiger roared in defiance as he approached the crying baby, intent on dispatching the boy in the same manner. Desperately, LaMotta inserted a fresh clip of bullets into his pistol. As he chambered a round, he felt a searing pain in his left shoulder. To his dismay, he saw a round hole in his vest with blood pouring from it. Looking straight ahead, he saw dozens of V.C. soldiers firing their weapons as they ran toward him. In the pandemonium, the alarmed tiger slipped into the jungle before he could harm the infant.

Feeling dizzy from the rapid loss of blood, LaMotta ignored the countless bullets that flew past, barely missing him, as he vainly lifted his son to carry him to one of the choppers. Despite the pleas of LaMotta's men, none of the copter pilots would wait for LaMotta and his child to board, given the grave risk of staying a moment longer.

Staggering, LaMotta held his son tightly as he lost consciousness, his last awareness that of the retreating choppers skirting the jungle canopy. In his coma-like state, he relived the Nam Demon viciously killing Sophie again and again. He relived the feeling of helplessness he felt as he saw the cat's gaping mouth and Sophie's blood dripping from it, and his devil eyes staring at LaMotta while he strutted arrogantly toward the baby.

Mercifully, LaMotta awoke, ending the nightmare. His eyes adjusted to a bright, bare light bulb that hung from a wooden beam overhead. Inspecting his surroundings, he thought it odd that the ceiling and walls were composed of earth. The air felt humid and musky.

A Vietnamese man of sixty entered the room nimbly, grinning widely. "Ah, Sergeant Bill, you awake. I take bullet out already. You no worry," said the man in a cordial voice.

"Where am I? Is my son all right? Please tell me, sir," LaMotta pleaded.

The man did not reply, but continued to smile as he dressed and placed a fresh bandage on LaMotta's wound.

"Sergeant Bill LaMotta," quipped a man of about thirty-five who had just entered the space, twirling LaMotta's dog tags. "You are in a tunnel. We have built thousands of miles of it to move troops about and protect us from your American big bombs. As for your son, he is being well cared for by my wife. It is fortunate for you and the boy she has good, full tits to feed both my son and your son," said a man named Tran in fluent English.

"Who are you?" asked LaMotta.

The man, who was only a few years older than LaMotta, did not reply immediately. Instead, he toyed with LaMotta's personal items, which they had taken from his pockets and spread out on a table. The Vietnamese man gazed intensely at the news clipping of LaMotta and the mother and cub tigers that he had slain. He then placed the clipping in his breast pocket. "I am Lieutenant Vu Tran, a soldier of the liberating North Vietnamese Army."

"Lieutenant Tran, I thank you for the care of my son," said LaMotta calmly, appearing to accept whatever fate would be dealt him as a prisoner of war.

Tran sat down on a chair, tapping his fingers on the table, staring at the prisoner and contemplating what to do with him, thinking LaMotta was more trouble than he was worth. "Sophie Nguyen, she was your woman?" asked Tran.

LaMotta breathed an amused sigh. "Sophie was as close as I was to any woman. I planned to take her and the boy back to the real world...uh, America."

"She was a North Vietnamese sympathizer. Sophie hid weapons and bombs for us," stated Tran.

At first LaMotta felt shock and disappointment that Sophie had lied to him about the weapons found in her hut. "Bitch. Oh, what the hell. We all fight for what we believe in, but I do not believe in shit. That makes her better than me. I would have taken her and our son back to Montana, anyway."

Tran bent over, pressing the palm of his hand heavily upon LaMotta's shoulder wound, causing him to grimace in pain. "You American soldiers are so arrogant. You are not welcome in Nam. You rape and murder our women and children." Tran's eyes seared with anger as he pulled the news clipping from his shirt pocket. He held it up to LaMotta's face. "The Nam Demon killed your woman. I think he did not kill Sophie at random. You keep this news photo for a reason. Is this the demon's mate and cub you killed for sport?" Tran said with gritted teeth.

LaMotta suspected Tran already knew the answer, but replied nonetheless. "Yes, I killed them. I am a hunter. I enjoy blasting anything that crawls, walks, swims, or flies. But shooting a female tiger and the cub she was protecting was probably not one of my best days of hunting."

Tran spit in LaMotta's face. "Stupid American. You awakened an evil spirit. This explains why the tiger will not leave. He waits for you. He has already slaughtered our chickens and cattle, and killed one of our men while he was protecting his goat herd. All of this trouble because of an American's foolishness."

LaMotta painfully sat up, fighting back guilt for all the trouble he had caused Tran's people. "Sophie's father said the tiger—uh, evil spirit—only sought revenge on us American assholes for raping your country, and me especially after I murdered his woman and son. He doesn't hurt you yellows," quipped LaMotta.

Tran cackled, shaking his head. "We 'yellows' bleed like you asshole American's do. If the demon wants a meal of chicken or beef, he will kill whatever stands in his way. My brother Chee is a skillful hunter and will kill the evil spirit for you."

Speaking no further, Tran left the room. LaMotta could hear him barking orders to his subordinates in another tunnel chamber in his local language. A moment later two men dressed in the plain beige uniforms of the North Vietnamese Army ran in, brandishing metal-tipped bamboo sticks. They began to brutally beat LaMotta across his entire body.

Instinctively, LaMotta rolled into a fetal position on the ground, covering his head with his hands and arms. A loud crack of his ribs breaking echoed along the length of the tunnel. The pain was more intense than anything LaMotta had ever endured in his life. The soldiers stopped when he was close to passing out. They fashioned a noose from coiled rope and threw a wide loop over LaMotta's head, cinching it tightly around his neck—so tightly as to nearly choke him. The soldiers pulled LaMotta through a maze of tunnel passageways like some disobedient dog. Exhausted and hurt, LaMotta would stumble, only to be dragged along. Fighting for each breath, he would wedge his fingers between the noose and his throat.

Upon exiting the tunnel, LaMotta became blinded by the brilliant tropical sun. His eyes came into focus, and he saw that he was in the middle of a small village, not unlike the one he had just ordered his men to raze. LaMotta was led to a small bamboo cage positioned near a footpath which led out of the village. There two soldiers began to undress him. Not wanting to risk another beating, LaMotta stood silently without resistance as he was stripped completely, with the exception of the bloody bandage that was wrapped around his left shoulder.

One soldier opened the cage, motioning with his hand for LaMotta to enter. Exhausted and in pain, he squeezed his tall, lanky body into the tiny cubicle. The soldier locked the cage door behind him with a heavy chain and padlock.

LaMotta stretched out his six-foot-plus frame on the reed mat. The cage was so minute that his feet and ankles stuck out between the bamboo bars. No food or water was given to him that day.

Awakened by the morning sun, LaMotta rose from a fitful sleep. His mouth and throat were parched. He coughed vigorously to work up enough saliva to moisten his cracked lips. He was surprised and embarrassed by his nakedness when he saw a group of village children standing nearby, staring at him silently.

"Goddamn gook brats, get outta my sight!" LaMotta shouted.

Although the children didn't understand English, it was obvious the strange man was angry at them, and they scattered quickly.

LaMotta buried his head in his hands in despair, fighting to keep his sanity. He felt a soft tapping on his arm. He raised his head. Standing beside the cage was a small boy of five. His tiny arms and hands extended through the spaces between the bamboo bars, offering a tin cup of water in one hand and a bright-red tropical fruit in the other.

LaMotta's hands trembled as he accepted the boy's offerings. Quickly the lad ran off, wearing the kind of innocent smile only small children possess.

"Kid, thanks!" LaMotta shouted. He heartily drank the water and ate the overly ripe fruit with gusto. The nourishment helped to clear his mind as he leaned back against the bamboo rods and observed the daily routines of the villagers. An elderly man threw bird scratch to his chickens; children, like children everywhere, played, not yet burdened by the problems of adults; women prepared breakfast for their families. Watching the normalcy of daily life allowed LaMotta, if only temporarily, to forget the dire straits he was in.

He saw Tran exiting a hut with another man with similar facial features and of similar age. Approaching the cage, the two men laughed while making idle chatter. Reaching the cage, Tran introduced his companion.

"Ugly American, I wish to introduce to you my brother Chee. He is a master hunter. From age twelve on my brother has provided the family with plenty of deer and wild pig. He will kill the Nam Demon for you. Then your only worry will be me," giggled Tran.

LaMotta eyed Chee with disdain. The man returned the stare with a cocky, self-assured grin.

"Sir, you have an American sniper's rifle slung over your shoulder. It looks like a model 70 Winchester .270 caliber with telescopic sites and a floating barrel. A fine gun for killing men, but such a weapon would not have enough balls to kill a 600-pound man-killer. I will not ask how you obtained the gun," LaMotta chuckled.

Tran appeared equally amused. "American, you are a naked prisoner sitting in a bamboo cage. Whether my brother has enough gun to kill the demon should be the least of your worries."

LaMotta nodded his head. "So true, Lieutenant. May I at least see my son before I die of starvation, disease, torture, or whatever else you may have in mind to kill me?"

The two men casually walked away without reply.

LaMotta slumped back down on the mat. The minutes and hours passed tediously slow. On occasion, the village boy brought him what food and water he could spare.

On the second morning of his captivity, LaMotta was awakened again by the sun. He rubbed the sleep from his eyes. In the soft earth inches from the cage he saw the footprints of the Nam Demon. He felt no fear or surprise. The beast could have easily killed him while he slept. "Like a goddamn cat who plays with a mouse before eating it, the son of-a-bitch tiger is toying with me before I become his dinner," LaMotta reflected.

Two more days passed. The circumstances and his injuries made it difficult for him to sleep, but LaMotta would see the huge paw prints of the demon each morning without ever laying eyes on the striped cat.

In late afternoon he would watch Tran's brother pass by, each time bearing the dejected look of an unsuccessful hunter.

"Master hunter! What bullshit. Your evil spirit has passed through the village center under your nose for the last three nights. Set me free, asshole, and I'll show you how to kill that fricking evil spirit," LaMotta shouted to Chee as he passed by empty handed. He knew Chee did not understand English, but he wanted to vent his frustration nonetheless.

On the fourth morning there were no fresh tracks from the demon. Instead, something else caught his attention. The busy villagers were no longer attired in dull peasant clothing, but rather the young and old alike were clothed in immaculate while muslin jackets and pants. They wore pillbox hats on their heads. An impromptu musical band carrying gongs and drums set up in the village square and began to practice vociferously. Understanding a little of the Vietnamese customs, LaMotta knew white represented death, and the long strands of firecrackers that were being hung from tall poles indicated a funeral ceremony.

LaMotta saw Sophie's father and Tran giving directions to the villagers preparing for the ceremony. It was obvious to LaMotta who the deceased person was they planned to honor.

"Mr. Nguyen, Tran, please let me out to pay my respects to Sophie," LaMotta said, resting on his knees, as the cage was too low for him to stand fully upright.

Tran walked to the cage carrying a pail of dishwater. "American, you have destroyed my Nam brothers' and sisters' homes and created a bastard that my people will shun." Tran flung the dishwater at LaMotta, drenching him with the dirty liquid.

"Bastard slant eye. When I am free of this cage I will kill you and piss on your body."

Tran crouched down to look LaMotta directly in the eyes. "American, you will kill no one. You will die in your little prison," he retorted.

"Goddamn gook. I'll kill you. I'll find a way," LaMotta shouted, dripping with foul-smelling water. "Devil cat, please kill me. You would be doing me a favor by putting me out of my misery," he uttered under his breath.

LaMotta cursed and ranted for several minutes until an elderly woman stepped out from a hut, cradling his son. The child was dressed in white silk stitched by an ancient, foot-pedaled sewing machine. On the boy's left ankle was a solid gold band, and his head was covered with a white hood to signify the child's virginity and purity. LaMotta gazed at the child that he yearned to hold. He wanted strongly to believe the boy was indeed his son.

"Perhaps Bill Jr. is or isn't my son. It no longer matters. No other American asshole has claimed him as his own. It ain't right that the kid shouldn't have a father," said LaMotta quietly. He smiled when he thought the boy might have looked in his direction.

The boy was taken back into the hut. LaMotta observed the village men stacking bundles of cut branches chest high. He surmised it was a funeral pyre for Sophie's cremation. Elsewhere, he watched a pig being slaughtered, to later be roasted over a flaming pit, while old women sang and folded colorful paper into fanciful decorations.

When the sun floated high overhead, and after hours of preparation, the musicians began the ceremony by banging their gongs and beating their drums. Strings of firecrackers, as long as two tall men, were lit. An ox cart entered the square, escorted by Tran, Sophie's father, and wailing mourners, some who were paid to mourn. On the cart lay Sophie, resting on a bed of fragrant jungle flowers. Her face was covered with a white cloth. Old women burned paper money over small fires in brass pots.

Despite his tragic circumstance, LaMotta could not help but feel pride and awe over Sophie's grand send-off. Sophie's father removed the cloth covering his daughter's face. Sobbing, he kissed her on the lips. Sophie was dressed in a fine silk dress. A scarf had been tied over her throat to hide the hideous wound made by the tiger, and her face was covered with heavy makeup, giving the appearance that Sophie was merely sleeping peacefully.

Although LaMotta didn't believe in God, he briefly bowed his head and closed his eyes, praying to no entity in particular that Sophie would go to a better place.

With great care, the father and three other village men placed Sophie's body on the pyre. A monk, one of a dozen wearing colorful robes from a local temple, lit the pyre as he and the others chanted.

"Goodbye, Sophie," LaMotta whispered as flames and smoke engulfed the corpse.

Watching the spectacle, LaMotta noticed a slight rustling of foliage on the nearby hillside, followed by quick blurs of orange through the patchwork of leaves and branches. He knew immediately it had to be the demon. He cried out frantically, trying to warn everyone, but the deafening noise of the clanging gongs, drums, and the firing of thousands of firecrackers drowned out LaMotta's warnings.

The big cat walked with an odd casualness among the preoccupied mourners. The small, fidgeting children were the first to notice the demon cat. Screaming wildly, they ran off in terror. Mourners scattered in all directions. Tran and Chee sprinted to their huts for weapons.

Unafraid, the tiger watched the fleeing villagers as he searched for LaMotta's son. Frustrated that he did not see the boy, the cat roared a chilling cry. He stepped to the pyre with an arrogant gate, and sniffed and licked at the air, his eyes searching for the infant. Standing a scant twenty paces from LaMotta, their eyes locked on each other. Both sets of eyes burned with hatred, and LaMotta knew the tiger could kill him if he so chose.

Tran and Chee raced out of their huts, firing their weapons blindly. The tiger leaped, unharmed, into the shifting pyre smoke. The two men separated, going on either side of the pyre. As LaMotta witnessed the surreal scene, he remembered the way the devil cat had taken advantage of the smoke when he had slain two of LaMotta's men the day he ordered the village to be burned to the ground. In horror, he watched Chee enter the wall of dense smoke in hot pursuit of the tiger.

"Stop! Don't pursue the cat in the smoke!" LaMotta screamed.

Chee didn't understand English, but given the heat of the moment, it was not likely he would have heard LaMotta's plea even if he had. A few silent moments passed, then Chee's weapon fired a long burst, emptying the clip.

"Chee! Did you get the tiger?" Tran asked, standing on the edge of the dense smoke. Staying alert, Tran waited for the smoke to shift.

Only a few seconds passed, but it seemed much longer before finally a gentle breeze changed the direction of the smoke. Chee was lying face down in a pool of blood. Tran flipped his body over, and saw that his throat had been ripped out, just as Sophie's had been. Chee's trigger finger was pressed stiffly on the trigger, which had caused the gun to fire involuntarily after he had died. Tran cradled his beloved brother against his chest. A defiant roar echoed through the highlands as the devil cat retreated over the hilltop.

Tran looked toward the horizon, too stunned to speak or display emotion as he listened to the Nam Demon. Prying the weapon from his brother's hand, he lifted his brother's body, shouting to the villagers that the demon had left and it was safe to return. He called for his wife, his mother, and LaMotta's child, who had sought safety in a tunnel, to come out.

In small groups, the villagers cautiously returned to the village. Once aware they had a second person to mourn, they gathered around Tran, who held Chee in his arms. Many were sobbing as they offered their sympathies to Tran. Friends and relatives carried Chee to a cave in a side hill, where the cool air would slow deterioration of the body until they could prepare another elaborate funeral.

Tran, his white silk clothing now painted a bright red from his brother's blood, spoke in his highland native tongue. He commanded a boy to bring him a sharp machete. In eager obedience, the child delivered the long-bladed knife to Tran. Holding the knife, Tran fondled the sharp edge, his mind so deep in thought that he didn't notice that he had cut his fingers on the razor-like edge. Slowly, Tran walked to LaMotta's cage.

Watching Tran approach, LaMotta felt mixed emotions toward him. Tran was his enemy, who had brutalized him savagely, but still, he had a grudging respect for him, who, like LaMotta, was a soldier. But, unlike LaMotta, Tran fought for strong beliefs, whereas LaMotta had become a soldier to escape his demons.

Reaching the cage, Tran raised the machete high over his head in a menacing manner. LaMotta looked up at Tran. "One less gook," blurted LaMotta defiantly, referring to Tran's brother Chee.

He expected to be hacked to death, and glared at Tran without flinching. With a swift, powerful chop, Tran began to cut the bindings that held the bamboo cage together until the wooden bars that imprisoned LaMotta collapsed in a jumbled pile.

"American bastard, stand up and join the living," said Tran.

LaMotta's legs felt like they were made of soft rubber after four days in his cramped prison. Tran caught LaMotta as he started to fall, holding him upright. LaMotta held his arm over Tran's shoulder, and the two of them walked to Tran's dwelling. Inside the hut, Tran placed LaMotta on a chair. LaMotta was a pitiful sight. Maggots crawled in his open wounds, and he reeked of urine and feces. Tran placed a cup in LaMotta's hand, then poured whiskey into it.

"Jack Daniel's! How did you get hold of such expensive whiskey?" LaMotta queried.

"American fool, it is your bottle. One of my men found it in your tent. It is one of the few good things you round-eyes have brought to my homeland," Tran chuckled.

Tran threw LaMotta a blanket to cover his naked body. He then placed a chair next to LaMotta, pouring himself a cup of whiskey. LaMotta gulped the whiskey as if it were water. Leaning back on the chair, Tran took small sips from his cup.

"American, you have caused my people so much misery. The demon killed Chee to get to you. So tell me, why did he not kill you?"

LaMotta extended his cup, indicating he needed a second drink. Tran poured another generous measure into his cup.

LaMotta took a long swallow, then replied, "Soldier boy, I am responsible for all the trouble I've caused you and your freakin' friends and relatives, but I will not apologize. It's called war. It's our job to make misery. As for why the demon did not kill me...there is more to it. The demon visited me every night I sat in that stinking, goddamn cage. I think it would have spoiled his fun to kill me too quickly. Besides, the devil cat, like me, is a hunter. It is not sporting to kill a game animal sitting in a cage."

Tran tossed his whiskey in LaMotta's face. "Round-eyed asshole. You must answer for my brother Chee. You were a hunter in your country. Together we will hunt down the Nam Demon, and together we will kill it," Tran said.

LaMotta wiped the whiskey from his face and licked his hand. "And when the demon is dead, you will set me and my son free?" he asked.

Tran shook his head. "My apologies, ugly American. My president, Ho Chi Minh, will not allow the release of POWs. He needs you for leverage. The more of you we have in cages, the more likely your President Johnson will want to stop fighting us."

LaMotta shook his head, cackling with amusement. "What is the point of helping you if you will not set my son and me free?"

"Silly American. I think hunting is important to you, as it was to my brother. Killing the Nam Demon will be your greatest trophy. I promise to take you out of a cage and place you in a more proper confinement. And lastly, you will be able to see your son whenever you wish," said Tran, knowing it would be difficult for a dedicated hunter to turn down such a challenging hunt. He took a sip of whiskey, smiling wryly. "If you refuse, I will put you in another cage, only this time, a smaller one, and I will place your son in a clearing in the jungle so the demon can kill him in exchange for the son you took from him."

LaMotta took offense at Tran's threats, but he had little choice in the matter. He nodded his head slowly in agreement. Tran then swallowed the remaining whiskey in his cup, poured more whiskey into LaMotta's cup, then refreshed his own. He raised his cup, as did LaMotta, and the two cups met in a toast.

"Death to the Nam Demon," said Tran.

"Death to the Nam Demon," mimicked LaMotta.

Tran ordered LaMotta out into the courtyard. Under a large tree stood two teenage girls holding clean towels. On a thick branch a makeshift shower was rigged—a perforated bucket beside a short ladder. One giggly girl directed LaMotta under the bucket, while the other giddy girl stood on the ladder and poured warm water into it. With soap and a face towel, the girls vigorously scrubbed the filth from LaMotta's body as water rained down on him.

LaMotta felt mixed emotions, cackling euphorically at the attention of the two nubile girls running their hands over his naked body, but subconsciously he was anxious about the truth that he was still a prisoner, and concerned whether Tran would keep his word and LaMotta would be treated better and allowed to see his son. LaMotta sensed Tran's contempt for him, and probably for all Americans. Tran was just humoring him, but he had few options but to hunt the tiger.

Refreshed and toweled dry, LaMotta was escorted to a hut where the maggots were dug out of his wounds, and medication (of which the villagers had little to spare) was applied and the wounds bandaged. An elderly woman shaved his week-old beard with a straight-razor.

After a hearty meal, the girls took LaMotta to another hut. Inside sat a polished brass bed, its mattress filled with fine goose down—a souvenir of a French land baron from Nam's colonial days. The girls giggled and pointed to the bed, indicating that he should rest. Though his injuries still caused him discomfort, the smell of clean cotton bed sheets and the gentle breeze created from hand-held paper fans that the girls waved on either side of his bed gave LaMotta a sense of serenity that he hadn't felt since leaving Montana, and his hunts alone in the Bitterroots, sitting beside a campfire at sunset, listening to the howling wolves. It was one of the few times in his life that his soul was truly free. In a dream, he envisioned his son, now a grown man, hunting elk in his beloved Montana.

Unable to breathe, LaMotta abruptly awakened. Returning to reality, he scanned his surroundings to see the two girls sleeping in chairs, exhausted after hours of waving their fans to make his sleep as comfortable as possible. The dream was deeply disturbing to LaMotta, who was puzzled as to why he didn't accompany his son on the hunt. Gazing out a glassless window, he saw the rose-orange colors of the rising sun. He had slept for fourteen hours.

The girls, awakened by his stirring, and with the usual giddiness of teenage girls, giggled. They spoke with their hands that they would soon return with breakfast and clothes. LaMotta smiled and bowed his head politely, reflecting that, not too many years ago, he had been their age, but it felt that so much more time had passed.

Still naked, he stood at the window, watching the sunrise. He questioned whether he had the right to kill the Nam Demon. LaMotta had been a sport hunter his entire life, and like most hunters, it was difficult to explain or justify why he felt such pride and joy in killing animals. But of course, he did not pursue the Nam Demon for sport. Before he could answer his own question, the girls returned with hot tea and fresh steamed pork bows. One of the girls carried LaMotta's combat clothing, cleaned and neatly folded, as well as his boots.

The girls turned their backs to him as he dressed in silly modesty, knowing they had seen him naked for the past four days. Sitting at a small table, the three of them smiled and cackled like good friends as they shared a fine meal.

With a rude intrusion, Tran entered before they finished their breakfast. "Ugly American, it is time to face the devil and spit in his eye," he said, tossing Chee's sniper rifle onto the table.

Shooing the girls outside, LaMotta inspected the rifle. "Two-seventy caliber, as I guessed," he said as he looked through the scope, adjusting it to its lowest power to better aim at the tiger at close range in consideration of the thick vegetation they would be hunting in.

"We leave now," Tran said, packing his own weapon of preference, an American Navy Winchester, model 12, 12-gage shotgun loaded with large lead slugs.

LaMotta chambered a round and slung the rifle over his shoulder. As Tran began to walk out the door, he pointed an index finger toward the emerald green hills, indicating the direction they would be going.

"Lieutenant, do you have a plan?" LaMotta asked.

"We find the demon's tracks and his shit, then stalk into range for a killing shot," Tran said confidently.

LaMotta cleared his throat, resisting the urge to laugh. "Lieutenant, I have tracked deer and elk in Montana, but Nam is not Montana. This goddamn jungle is so thick you can't see your hand if you extend it out from your body."

Tran chambered a round and pointed the shotgun at LaMotta's head. "American, you are my prisoner. We hunt my way."

LaMotta was unsure whether Tran would actually pull the trigger, but he didn't want to find out. "Let's go kill a devil," he said matter-of-factly.

Tran pushed the safety on his gun, then put the shotgun over his shoulder. Saying nothing more, the two men walked with a fast gate toward the hills.

The two men traversed the steep terrain every minute of the available daylight, not stopping to eat and only drinking water when they crossed an occasional small stream. Nearing sundown, they at last came upon fresh tiger tracks, but in the growing darkness, they decided to end the hunt and resume the next day. To their chagrin, they found tiger tracks on top of their own footprints in the soft earth on their return journey to the village.

A great uneasiness grew in both men, knowing the cat could have attacked them in the dense jungle, but chose not to. Nevertheless, Tran informed LaMotta they would use the same strategy the following day.

In the fading light, Tran's wife and mother greeted the two men with a warm embrace. Inside Tran's dwelling was LaMotta's son, sleeping contently in a cradle being rocked by Sophie's father. Tran allowed LaMotta to hold the infant for a moment. LaMotta kissed him softly on the lips. He yearned to end the hunt and go back to the real world with Bill Jr. Strangely, LaMotta felt a bit of hatred toward the tiger. Surely he wanted to kill the beast, as did Tran, but he was not obsessed with it as Tran was in retaliation for the killing of his brother.

"The devil cat has killed Sophie and three of my men, but I cannot buy or steal yesterday back, not even if I kill a hundred tigers," said LaMotta under his breath as he placed the baby back into the cradle.

The two men sat down to a pleasant dinner of native foods and homemade beer. Both Tran and LaMotta viewed each other with inherent distrust and prejudice, but gradually the strong beer broke away the invisible wall that separated them. They swapped hunting stories of their youth in their respective homelands. After several beers, LaMotta thought what a fine hunting companion Tran would have made had they not been born a world apart.

After dinner, LaMotta fell into a sound sleep on the comfortable brass bed, fully aware of the armed guards posted outside. In the morning, the two girls awakened LaMotta long before the first rays of the morning sun. Tran joined LaMotta in wolfing down a quick breakfast, then they began another long hike into the surrounding hills.

With LaMotta in the lead, they trudged in a zigzag pattern, searching for the slightest sign of the tiger. Soon both men were drenched with perspiration, and leeches clung stubbornly to their heads and bodies. On and on they walked with slow, deliberate steps, neither willing to admit the demon had them outwitted.

By late afternoon the men had not found even the slightest sign of the tiger. LaMotta whispered to Tran that they needed a new strategy. Before Tran could answer, a half-dozen gunshots rang out from the direction of the village. The two men sprinted away as fast as the dense undergrowth would allow them. As they neared the village, they could make out all of the able-bodied men in a circle around the village, armed with antiquated World War I English rifles, axes, or pitchforks.

"What happened?" Tran shouted as they approached.

"The demon was here. Some of the men fired at the evil spirit, but he escaped unharmed," explained a village elder.

Tran's wife pushed her way through the frightened villagers who gathered together in a tight group. Sobbing, she wrapped her arms around Tran.

"Did the demon harm anyone, or attack the cattle?" he asked.

His wife shook her head. "No, my husband. The spirit attacked none of our people and no livestock." She then looked at Tran with a more significant fear than the time she'd fled in terror from American bombings. "It was all so horrible. The demon walked toward me as I drew water from the village well. Our son was strapped to my back. I dared not look into the spirit's eyes for fear he would steal my soul. He could have killed me and our son with ease, but did not. Perhaps he was scared off when the village men came to my aid. I feared not so much for myself, but for our son's safety," she said, her voice quivering.

"My dear wife, I will not allow the demon to harm you or our son. I will have my own soldiers guard you day and night until I kill the demon, this I promise you," Tran said.

Tran ordered two of his most trusted soldiers to guard his wife and son. He then ordered LaMotta to follow him to a vacant hut for a private conversation.

"Sit," he commanded.

LaMotta sat on a wicker chair, as ordered.

Tran sat down beside him, his elbow on his knee, his chin resting in the palm of his hand. His mind wrestled for an answer to killing the demon. "The Nam Demon waltzed through the village while we two fools were sweating and bleeding through the highlands, but yet the demon did not kill anyone in the village."

LaMotta chuckled. "Lieutenant, there was only one fool. I told you, I warned you, crawling through the thick jungle would not even get you an ass's hair of that devil cat."

Tran nodded. "All right, ugly American. You were right, I was wrong. But now I make the correct decision. You will be the bait. The demon wants you. That is why he did not kill anyone in the village."

LaMotta grinned and shook his head. "No way. The fricking cat could have killed me in the jungle on the first day of our hunt. No fricking way!"

"Sergeant LaMotta, you are the expert hunter. You wisely said the cat plays with the mouse before devouring it."

"Lieutenant, like you I am not always right," LaMotta said with a sarcastic tone.

Tran's face flushed red with anger. He struck LaMotta on the face so hard that he fell backwards off the wicker chair. "American trash, you will be the bait. You owe it to my brother."

LaMotta sat up on the floor and wiped the blood from his lower lip. "Why should I owe your brother anything? I only had the pleasure of meeting the nice man a few days ago."

Tran bent down and grasped LaMotta's collar. "Chee was Sophie's husband. You owe him," he said, enunciating each word distinctly.

"How did Sophie end up in Saigon?" LaMotta asked with a tone of indifference.

Tran placed a cigarette in his mouth and lit it with a Zippo lighter he had confiscated from a dead American soldier. He hated to discuss his sister-in-law, and needed a cigarette to calm himself. "Seven years ago my sister-in-law grew tired of relieving herself in a hole in the ground and laboring in the terraced rice fields. Her face and hands were turning into sun-baked leather. She left for Saigon to become a whore. Chee didn't know she returned to her home village until after the demon killed her. If I were not a Communist, I would be thanking the Lord Buddha that Chee did not die knowing the whore and her bastard son would be going with you to the country of white devils." He inhaled a long drag

47

from his cigarette. "Chee was a lost soul when Sophie left him. You owe him."

LaMotta looked unmoved. "I didn't know your brother except when he would pass me as I sat in my cage to hunt that damn orange cat. I could have told him how to kill your freaking evil spirit had he asked me. There was a mountain lion back in Montana that kept feasting on my neighbor's cattle. I slew that evil spirit by staking a young, tender calf in a meadow. I dispatched him the first night of the hunt. I will be your calf for Sophie, but for Chee, never."

"American son-of-a-bitch. Like all round-eyes, you destroy peoples' lives without remorse. I will not cry if the demon tears your throat out as he did my brother's. Sleep for a few hours. We begin the hunt at midnight," Tran said.

Returning to his hut, LaMotta was greeted warmly by the two girls, who tended to his needs. On the table sat steamed fish, rice, and bok choy. LaMotta dismissed the girls. Having no appetite, he blew out the candles and lay on the brass bed. Unable to sleep, he rested with eyes wide open. He knew he had lived an empty life. He chuckled over Tran's comment that he would not shed a tear if the tiger killed him. "Actually, no one would shed a tear over my death. Maybe I do owe Tran's brother," he said under his breath. *If only I could have taken my son back to the real world and given him a good life. It would have at least been one life I would not have ruined*, he thought, lying in the pitch-black room.

At midnight, Tran came for LaMotta to begin a hunt where the line between the hunter and the hunted was becoming blurred. Knowing the obvious danger he was placing himself in, LaMotta requested that he be allowed to see his son for a moment. His son spent most nights in the hut of Sophie's father who, like LaMotta, had difficulty sleeping. Distrusting all white devils, Sophie's father reluctantly allowed LaMotta to enter his hut. LaMotta stepped softly so as not to awaken his son. The child had an ironic sense of serenity as he slept, considering all the turmoil and anguish that revolved around his young life.

LaMotta lightly touched the infant's cheek with his fingers. "Bill, my son, I would give my left nut to take you to Montana, to hike the mountains together and be there when you bag your first mule deer buck," he whispered.

An impatient Tran stomped into the hut, informing LaMotta that it was time to leave. Hesitating, LaMotta whispered, "Goodbye," to his son, then walked away with Tran.

Although Tran carried a flashlight, he hiked without turning it on, LaMotta following close behind in the black night to a clearing in the jungle. Tran ordered LaMotta to sit in the middle of the clearing. The plan was for Tran to lie in wait on the edge of the jungle. Once the tiger entered the clearing to attack LaMotta, Tran would act swiftly by turning on the flashlight, illuminating his target, then making a killing shot to the tiger's head.

"Don't miss," whispered LaMotta in a half-joking, half-serious tone.

He placed the pillow given to him by the two girls on the ground, then sat on it, unarmed. With legs crossed, he sat motionless as mosquitoes drilled incessantly into every exposed part of his body. Soon his entire body ached, but whatever discomfort and pain LaMotta felt could not compete with his growing anxiety and fear of the demon's attack. The vision of Sophie's throat being torn out viciously repeated in his mind over and over, as did the image of bright blood spewing everywhere.

He thought of Tran perhaps falling asleep or missing the shot when the tiger did attack. Like a frightened boy whistling in the dark, he assured himself that Tran was an expert shot with steady nerves.

One hour, then two, then three passed in the still black of night. There was no hint of the tiger in the vicinity.

The popping of a light caliber pistol streaked from the village, breaking the long monotony. Tran leaped to his feet and sprinted back to the village, leaving LaMotta behind in the clearing.

"Asshole, wait for me!" LaMotta shouted as he struggled to stand, his legs numb from hours of sitting in one position. He thought it odd that Tran would leave him unsupervised, but reasoned Tran knew he would not try to escape and leave his son behind.

LaMotta began to slap his thighs forcefully to return circulation to his legs. Walking briskly at first, he started to run as the blood flow returned to his legs. Stumbling and crashing over rocks and ground vines, practically blind in the unlit night, he paused to listen, focusing his ears and mind. He heard the faint noise of Tran hurrying through the undergrowth as he headed back to the village.

LaMotta raced in the direction of the faint sounds. Without the aid of a flashlight, he fought back bushes covered with sharp thorns and stinging nettles, until he saw the campfires from the village in the distance. Realizing he was headed in the right direction, he ran even faster, his only thought that of his son's safety.

When he reached the village, LaMotta was aghast to see the villagers crowded around the hut belonging to Sophie's father. Near the entrance was a body covered with a blood-soaked blanket, partially obscured by the mourners who kneeled around it.

"Please, no! Tiger, you should have taken me, not my son!" LaMotta exclaimed.

Tran stepped out of the hut, followed by his wife, who held LaMotta's son. Relieved to see that his son was unharmed, LaMotta took the infant into his arms and held him with great care.

"Sophie's father is dead," said Tran. "He gave his life defending his grandson with a small pistol he owned. The demon left a few droplets of blood as he fled, but the villagers who saw the spirit flee say he moved with strong vigor, so his wounds are not serious."

LaMotta shook his head. "Lieutenant, I am sorry the old man is dead. My son would be dead were it not for the old man's bravery."

"Tu Nguyen was a good and honorable man. That is why I gave him this dwelling after you burned his home down. It was he who offered to guard your son, even though he hated the tainted blood of Americans, as most of my people do."

LaMotta hung his head shamefully, not knowing how to reply.

Tran poked LaMotta in the chest with contempt. "The demon does not want you, he wants your son. And eye for an eye, as you American assholes say. We will begin another hunt in the morning, this time using your son as bait. This time the evil spirit will come to us," Tran said.

LaMotta backed away a few paces, holding his son protectively, just as the demon's mate had protected her cub when he had killed both of them. "Bullshit. You cannot have my son as bait," he exclaimed.

Tran pulled his pistol, extending his arm straight out, and pointing it directly at LaMotta's head. He ordered his men to aim their weapons at LaMotta, as well.

"Ugly American, my men and I will kill you here and now, and your bastard son will still be used as bait. If you give him to me, you will be beside me to back me up when I kill the demon."

With hesitation, LaMotta handed his son to Tran. "Lieutenant Tran, if the goddamn tiger kills my boy, I will kill you," he threatened.

Tran grinned with amusement. "You arrogant American bastards have tried to kill me for a long time, and before that the French bastards tried to kill me. We leave at daybreak. You rest for a few hours." He paused. "American, I need your word that you will not try to run with your son," he added as an afterthought.

LaMotta nodded his head in compliance.

In the pale moonlit night the two men, with the infant in

tow, began a two-mile hike along a narrow trail. The chest-high grass danced in the warm breeze. It reminded LaMotta of the flatlands in Montana where he and Joe hunted ducks.

"That goddamn cat could jump our asses at any time out of this shit," mumbled LaMotta.

"What did you say, American?" asked Tran, turning his head.

LaMotta glared at Tran with exasperation. "I said the tiger could ambush us in this high grass."

Tran chuckled, amused by the remark. "Silly American. You did not protest yesterday when we could have been ambushed on the same trail."

"Yesterday I didn't carry my son," said LaMotta, becoming irate.

Tran stopped abruptly, wearing a gaze of equal anger. "Your colleagues in the sky dropped bombs on a village just across the border, killing my six-year-old son and his grandparents. I will shed no tears if the demon eats you or your son." He turned around and resumed walking.

LaMotta fought his inner demons, not wanting to feel any compassion for the man who was supposed to be his bitter enemy. "Bill, keep hating, you asshole. Keep hating to survive," he said to himself under his breath.

At first light the trio reached the clearing LaMotta had sat in the previous day. Nestled in a wicker basket was LaMotta's son. He placed the basket on the ground in the center of the clearing, kissing the child on his forehead. Then he dragged a blanket bearing the baby's scent in a zigzag pattern around the east end of the clearing. Creating what he felt would be more than enough scent to lure the tiger into their trap, LaMotta joined Tran in a planned spot on the edge of the clearing where Tran had cut the high grass down enough for them to sit, offering a clear shot to where the baby was, a mere thirty paces away.

Tran handed LaMotta his brother's sniper rifle. The two men sat together, LaMotta a couple of feet behind Tran, as

Tran insisted on taking the first shot.

Though the morning was still young, the hot, humid air clung to the men like a damp blanket. Sweat trickled down their faces. LaMotta had positioned his infant in the shadow of a tall oak that stood sentinel on the east edge of the clearing, but he knew that if the tiger didn't show by late morning, the shade would retreat, leaving the child vulnerable to the oppressive sun.

Time passed painfully slow, with no sign of the tiger. Visions of his nightmarish imprisonment in the bamboo cage flashed in LaMotta's mind. He wondered if Tran would be true to his word and not put him back in the cage after they had killed the tiger. But cage or no cage, he would still be a prisoner, and there was also the welfare of his son to consider. He had seen children of mixed American and Vietnamese descent being spit on and mocked in Saigon. The treatment of his son would perhaps be worse in the Communist north.

As the sun approached its zenith, he tried to push aside such thoughts and stay focused on the task at hand. Gradually, the sun's rays began to burn the child's face. The infant awoke crying, frightened and confused by the unfamiliar surroundings.

Speaking as softly as possible, LaMotta whispered to Tran that he be allowed to give his son water and comfort him briefly. Tran replied adamantly with a single word. "No." He glared at LaMotta harshly for a moment, then turned his head back toward the infant, believing the infant's loud sobs would be even more incentive for the demon to come into the ambush.

LaMotta could barely stand the child's suffering. He covered his ears with the palms of his hands, but it did little to drown out his son's wailing. He began to weigh his chances of surviving as a prisoner of war. Even if he would be treated more humanely, it might be years before he was released to go back to the real world.

"My son, it's time to go home," mouthed LaMotta. He lifted a nearby rock and struck Tran across the back of his head, rendering him unconscious. He ran to his son, snatching him up. He carried the boy past Tran, and stopped for a moment to gaze at the man lying face down in the dirt. The guilt and shame for his act was overwhelming. "My apologies, Lieutenant Tran. I would have enjoyed helping you kill that goddamn devil cat, but I cannot take the chance of going back to the cage or never seeing my son again."

With a farewell salute, LaMotta headed south with his son, hoping to be spotted by an American chopper on patrol.

Holding the basket close to his side, LaMotta ran with frenzied determination. After three-quarters of a mile he stopped, not so much from exhaustion, but to reflect on his priorities. Had he been right to strike Tran and flee? He placed the basket on the ground. Gingerly, he trickled droplets of water from his canteen into the child's mouth.

"My dear son, we must go back. I'm a hunter. I need to finish the hunt."

Running as quickly as he could back to the clearing, he glanced down at his son, who smiled at him as if amused by the bumpy ride. LaMotta returned a loving smile to his son. An odd sense of peace came over him as he sprinted back to the clearing.

"Billy boy, it's our first hunt together. I will kill the Nam Demon, then we will go to the real world. I will teach ya how to hunt," he said.

Crawling through the undergrowth with the basket in tow, he pushed into an opening. From fifty paces ahead he saw Tran sitting up, rubbing a large bump on his head. Relieved that he had not seriously harmed Tran, LaMotta stood up and quietly approached. He walked slowly to lessen the noise, but he was also nervous as to how he would excuse his assault and attempted escape. Tran's treatment toward him had been brutal, but he had given the man his word that he would not run. His word was one of the few virtues he adhered to in his life. His mind was knotted with different emotions—the thrill of the hunt for a dangerous animal was indeed an overriding thought. *The fricking cat did kill my woman and a whole lot of other people, but I drew first blood with his mate and cub. Which one of us deserves revenge more?* he thought.

Covering half the distance to Tran, LaMotta detected a flicker of orange in the dense foliage. Knowing immediately it had to be the demon, he cried out a warning at the same instant the tiger bolted out of the shadows. It pulled Tran to the ground before he could react to LaMotta's warning. The tiger struck his back, his claws sinking into Tran's ribs. LaMotta put down the basket and drew his gun. He fired a shot, trying to avoid hitting Tran. The .270 caliber bullet creased the top of the tiger's shoulder. The superficial wound directed the tiger's attention toward LaMotta before the beast could take Tran's life.

Instinctively, LaMotta ran forward, firing point-blank, putting distance between him and his son. He prayed the tiger wouldn't notice the child lying in the basket.

Three bullets exploded harmlessly into the soft earth, spraying soil into the tiger's face. A fourth bullet struck the tiger in the shoulder, severely wounding him, but not fatally. Angered, the demon roared in defiance, his ears laid back against his head, and strands of saliva dripping from his upper row of teeth.

His rifle now empty, LaMotta stood his ground. The two enemies glared at one another in anger as if the hunter and the hunted were cut from the same cloth. Their conflict transcended countless millennia. LaMotta stood like a statue. He had taken life in its many forms thousands of times. Now he was the prey. Like a mountain lion about to pounce on a yearling, there was no point in running.

"Nam Demon, I am your trophy," whispered LaMotta as the full weight of the tiger crashed upon him.

In one swift blur the beast viciously tore out LaMotta's jugular and windpipe. Blood spurted from LaMotta's neck like water from a broken pipe. Triumphantly, the Nam Demon licked the blood until LaMotta's heart gave out and the blood stopped flowing. Straddling the man's body, the tiger noticed the basket a short distance away. Smelling the infant's scent, he knew it was LaMotta's son. The tiger's thirst for retribution would not be quenched until he had killed LaMotta's only child. He limped toward the basket and stood over the infant. His eyes burned vengefully as he gazed at LaMotta's son, blood dripping from his mouth onto the child's bare stomach.

The child's eyes widened like saucers. He was too frightened to cry.

A loud boom reported from Tran's shotgun. A 500-grain slug slammed into the tiger's rump. Pivoting, the tiger charged Tran, gaining ground rapidly despite having the use of only three good legs. Tran pumped and fired the shotgun, placing four slugs into the cat's chest. The determined beast showed no reaction to the damaging hits. With the tiger nearly upon him, Tran shoved the muzzle of the gun barrel into the cat's mouth and fired the last round, finally taking the demon's life. The fourteen-foot long cat continued over Tran with forward momentum, bowling Tran over.

The tiger's limp body lay across Tran, gurgling a death groan. With great effort, Tran pushed the cat off him. Standing up, Tran's body shook with fear. He poked the end of his gun barrel into the cat's eye, looking for some reaction —a practice hunter's often use to make certain a downed game animal is indeed dead. Tran released a sigh of relief when the demon's eye did not blink.

"The Nam Demon, an evil spirit that cannot die," Tran said with a wry smile.

He walked a few yards to retrieve the infant. Both man and child smiled toward one another. Carrying the basket, Tran paused at LaMotta's body before returning to the village. The man's neck was grotesquely ripped apart.

"American bastard, I think you did not return for my

sake. I think perhaps to kill a trophy tiger was your only reason for returning, but I thank you anyway for saving my life. Goodbye, brave soldier." He bent down to close LaMotta's lifeless eyes.

Carrying LaMotta's child, Tran returned to the village. He ordered several of the village men to recover LaMotta's body, as well as the tiger's. When they returned, they paraded the tiger's body on a large wooden plank all around the village, while Tran was carried on the shoulders of the villagers with joyous pride. A lavish party was held in Tran's honor that lasted three days.

When the celebration had ended, LaMotta's body was cremated on a funeral pyre. His ashes were mixed with Sophie's ashes in an urn and placed amid grand ceremony in a cave which held the ashes of other family members. After much political maneuvering and paperwork, the International Red Cross delivered LaMotta's son to an American military base outside of Saigon. Captain Sevenson took immediate steps to adopt the child.

Six months later, Captain Sevenson retired from the military and returned to the real world of his native Michigan with his adopted son. He taught his son how to hunt, fish, and live off the land, knowing that LaMotta would have wanted the same for the boy.

With selective memory, exaggeration, and outright lies, Sevenson would instill in the boy his late father's bravery, his love for the Vietnamese people, and his love for Bill Jr. and his mother. Sevenson repeatedly told him throughout his childhood the story of his father's valiant, one-on-one battle with the Nam Demon to save the boy's life, as well as Tran's life, while giving his own. The only variation to the story was the size of the tiger and its number of victims in succeeding years.

When the boy turned thirteen, as a rite of passage Sevenson took him on his first elk hunt in the Bitterroots of Montana. After a long, skillful stalk on a spike elk, the boy took careful aim. He heard the voice of his father tell him to hold his breath as he pulled the trigger, placing the crosshairs a tad bit behind the elk's shoulder. The bullet hit true, killing the young bull in his tracks.

Together man and boy knelt beside the elk to speak a silent prayer of thanks to God for a successful hunt, and a thank you from the boy to the spirit of his father for giving him life.

When Bill Jr. graduated from high school, he moved to Montana to become a hunting guide. There he met a robust cowgirl who shared his love for hunting and the wild country. They had two sons. The boys would sit, mesmerized, on Bill's lap as he told them the story of their grandfather's battle with the Nam Demon.

In his early thirties, Bill took his family to Vietnam, where he visited his birthplace. He also visited his parents' burial site, where he took half of the blended ashes of his parents, leaving half in Sophie's homeland, and scattering the other half in his father's beloved Bitterroots.

Bill Jr. and his sons loved and revered Bill LaMotta, Sr., thinking of him as a perfect man, never knowing that the Nam Demon was not the only demon he battled in his life.

— The End —

Murder in Lotus Land

"Sid, why is this frickin' funeral band so loud?" Katie Sung shouted to her husband over the deafening noise.

"Katie, just be glad you're of French descent and not Chinese. This may be 1980, but old Chinese rituals and silly customs die hard here in China," explained Sidney Sung. "They're making such clamorous noise to let Heaven know that my grandfather is about to arrive."

"Well, considering how loud your grandfather used to shout at me, I wouldn't think he would need such a fanfare to let them know he's coming," Katie remarked facetiously. "Besides, how can they be sure which way he's going? I know very well your grandfather always resented his grandson marrying a *gwai lah,*" she added bitterly, using the Chinese phrase that was derogatory to Caucasians.

"Don't be silly!" Sidney said, tickling her ribs in jest. "He was fond of you, he just didn't like all those heavy French sauces you used to serve him."

"Shush!" snapped Julie, Sidney's grandmother. She gave her grandson a menacing look and pressed her index finger to her lips.

"Sorry, Nana," Sydney said. He gazed at his feet in embarrassment.

The body of patriarch Gun Sung and the long procession of mourners—many who were paid to make the funeral look more auspicious—wound through his hometown. His body lay in an open, expensive bronze casket. Spectators lining the streets of the small village named Lotus Land gawked at the native son lying in the casket. They spoke of how he'd left years ago to seek his fortune on the Gold Mountain—

America—and how splendid the gentleman looked in his tailored Western tuxedo.

As Chinese custom dictated, the procession stopped at the childhood home of the deceased, so that he might have one last look at his former residence. The dwelling was quite ordinary and plain, as were most of the buildings in Lotus Land. A wreath of bright-red roses—good luck for the Chinese—adorned the front entrance. Amid the loud wailing of the mourners, and the even louder unsynchronized music, Burt Sung, the eldest son of Gun Sung, removed the wreath from the front entrance and placed it gently upon the funeral wagon carrying his beloved father.

Fragrant Lotus Lilies were tossed into the open casket by mourners and bystanders alike. The village of Lotus Land, named for the myriad Lotus Lilies growing in the many ponds and lakes of the region, had not witnessed such an auspicious funeral since the death of the regional governor a few years earlier.

"Lotus! Lotus…" cried an elderly woman in Chinese. She pulled at the collar of the dead man's expensive tuxedo. The old woman was promptly thrown to the ground by one of the pallbearers. Katie helped the sobbing woman to her feet.

"Lotus…you have forgotten her!" the woman screamed as she was whisked away by burly members of the funeral procession.

"Who was that old woman?" Katie whispered to her husband. "Sid, why was she acting so ballistic?"

"No doubt a crazy woman. She was shouting something about a woman named Lotus, perhaps an old debt from years past that my grandfather neglected to pay. Whatever it was about, it's not important."

"Demented or not, that frail old woman should have been treated more respectfully," Katie lectured Sid.

"Goddamn it, Katie, what did you want us to do? That old woman means nothing to me. I don't care who Lotus is and I do not care to know who that decrepit old hag is, either." Sidney's lips tightened and he gritted his teeth. "We came here to bury my grandfather, remember?"

Katie gave her husband a cold, biting stare. She then picked up her pace in the procession to avoid speaking to him. A young boy of twelve held an umbrella over her blond head to shield her from the sweltering sun.

"Shay shay," Katie said, saying thank you with one of the few Chinese words she knew as she walked with the others on that hot August day.

A warm breeze only brought added offense to the smell of human excrement, used to fertilize the nearby rice fields. The smell assaulted the mourners' nostrils. Finally, after what seemed an eternity, the procession ended at the public city hall—a common meeting place for local villagers, and often used for funeral receptions. The large mass of mourners entered the dingy, off-white building, following the pallbearers and a young man carrying a large, blow-up photo of the deceased attached to a long pole.

"Coca Cola! God bless you, girl," Katie said gratefully as she accepted an ice-cold soft drink offered to her by a young girl.

The smell of burning incense helped reduce the obnoxious odor of the fertilizer that drifted into the immense hall. Almost as a reward, an elegant dinner awaited those who endured the exhausting and uncomfortable funeral walk, which was further exasperated by the obligatory black clothing that clung to their bodies.

"A toast to my beloved father!" yelled Burt Sung as he raised a glass of wine.

"Gun Sung! May you live forever in our hearts!" came the unified toast from the vociferous crowd, lifting wine bottles and glasses toward the ceiling.

"A pity Lotus is not living. She dearly loved parties, regardless of the purpose behind them."

The voice came from an old, distinguished-looking Chinese gentleman. His comment was directed to no one in particular, but Katie overheard.

"Sir, who was Lotus?" she inquired. "What was her relationship to Grandfather Gun?"

"Well, my pretty *lo fon*, a distant relative. Lotus was a—"

"Cousin Cheng! What a delight to see you again!" exclaimed Grandmother Julie, interrupting the old man before he could answer Katie's question. "Has it been twenty-five years? Please, come sit with me. We have much to catch up on!"

Katie's mouth dropped open in astonishment at Grandma Julie's rudeness. *How odd Nana Julie stole that old man away from me—as if she didn't want him to answer my questions,* Katie thought.

The tall, *lo fon* blond stood motionless in the middle of the large room, surrounded by a sea of black-clothed Chinese. A multitude of Chinese voices saturated the large hall.

"I don't belong here," Katie muttered under her breath as the day's events raced through her mind. "I love Sid very much, but perhaps I should not have come to China."

"Katie…Katie…" Sidney said, tapping her shoulder. Katie seemed to pay no attention. "Mrs. Sung, do you plan on not speaking to me for the rest of our lives? If so, you must allow me to get that dog I always wanted. At least then there will be someone to lick my face when I go to bed at night," he mused.

"Oh, Sid. You are the love of my life. I can't stay mad at you for long. Besides, you're the only one here who will speak to me." Katie gave her husband a hug.

"Nanking," said Sidney.

"Excuse me?"

"Nanking. Once we pay our respects and get acquainted with my relatives—who we've never even seen before and will never see again—we'll tour the historic walled city of Nanking. Then it will be on to Beijing to take more fuzzy photos. It will be like a second honeymoon, as well as a chance to show you the country of my ancestors," Sidney said with a wide grin.

"Wouldn't that be lovely, Sid? I would love for you to show me your beloved China. Hey, do you know an old man named Cheng?" Katie said, suddenly changing the subject. "That's him standing over there with Nana Julie. I believe he's your grandmother's cousin."

"Cheng is my great-granduncle's son, which makes him Nana Julie's cousin, as you've already determined. He was a lawyer before the Communist takeover. Then he spent the last thirty years raising chickens. It's an indoctrination of sorts, and a rehab of China's intellectuals. I'm just not sure how raising chickens is going to change a person's mind or soul. Why are you interested in grand cousin Cheng, anyway?"

"Nothing, Sid. Forget it," Katie said with a slight tone of frustration in her voice.

After two more days of feasting and idle chatter with Sidney's relatives, Sidney and Katie took off for the city of Nanking, once the provisional capital of China before the Communist takeover. Meanwhile, Sidney's parents, Burt and Grace, went on to Hong Kong to shop and sightsee with Grandmother Julie.

"The Japanese killed and raped thousands of my countrymen and women in the 1930s," Sid said as he and Katie stood atop the remains of the ancient wall that used to surround the city.

Katie took Sid's hand. "How dreadful, Sid. Why must some people be so cruel to others?" She spoke softly as they gazed at the panoramic view of the city. Her question went unanswered as a young boy approached.

"Paper! News! Please, you buy paper?" he said in broken English. He shoved a newspaper in Sidney's face.

"Stupid kid, take your business elsewhere!" snapped Sidney, brushing aside the newspaper waving in his face.

"Sid, buy the paper. Here—I have plenty of change in my purse," Katie said as she rummaged for loose change.

"Silly *gwai lah*, are you forgetting that the two of us cannot read Chinese?" chided Sidney. "What do you want us to do with it? Fold Origami?"

"Sid, this young boy is obviously destitute. Give him the money so he can eat for one more day." Katie placed a fistful of coins in Sidney's hands.

"Here, you bought the paper—you carry it," Sidney said, shoving the paper into Katie's hands.

Clutching the Chinese newspaper, Katie began to roll it up. "Holy shit!" Katie exclaimed. Her eyes widened in disbelief.

"What's wrong now?" Sidney asked with frustration.

"Look at this photo! The police are pulling the body of an old woman out of a river," Katie said excitedly.

"What of it?"

"Look closely," Katie said, handing Sid the paper. "It's the same old woman from the funeral. The one who made all of that commotion. She kept screaming about someone named Lotus—and now suddenly she's dead!"

"Dear wife, there are over a billion souls in China. Should it surprise you that thousands of people die on a daily basis?" Sidney said, slightly annoyed.

"Yes, my love, you are right—as always. People die every day, especially in China, which has endured 3,000 years of grief. Anyway," she continued, changing the subject, "we have an old college bud who now lives in Nanking. He works for UPI, I believe. I know he would be thrilled to see us. Let's pay him a visit."

"But you never even liked Tim Snider. You said he was a loud, obnoxious boor."

"People change," Katie said, grasping Sidney's hand and tugging him to the street to whistle for a taxi.

———

"Katie! You're still one sweet, awesome babe," yelled the

rotund Tim Snider. He squeezed Katie and attempted to give her a more than friendly kiss.

"Tim! Um…such a pleasure to see you, too," Katie said, catching her breath and pulling away from his python-like hold.

"Hey, excuse me, old college buddy. There is another living, breathing human standing here," Sidney said. He took offense toward his old college friend, who was not only ignoring him, but also showing overzealous signs of affection toward his wife.

"Sid, Sid, Sid. Sorry!" mused Tim. "Sorry. I would have given my old college buddy a big, wet kiss, but I figured Katie might have gotten jealous! Man, I forgot you were the one who taught me how to eat with chopsticks. That really helped me score with the Chinese chicks!" Tim gave Sidney an equally breath-robbing hug. "So, have a seat, you two, get comfy. What the hell brings you over to my place, anyway?" Tim motioned them toward the living room.

"Tim, I need a favor," Katie said, pointing to the article about the death of the old Chinese woman. "I'd like you to translate this article for us, please."

"Katie!" Sid exclaimed. "This is just too much. Forget the fucking old dead woman. Why is she such an obsession with you?" He snatched the newspaper from her hands.

"Sid, I didn't even want to come to China. I've told you several times: Your relatives treat me as if I'm nonexistent. Perhaps there is some poetic justice to it since the *gwai lahs* have looked down on your people for so long—but that's not *my* fault! So what if I want to know more about this "fucking old dead woman," as you refer to her. I feel like it gives me some kind of purpose for being here. I'd like to be more than just an attractive ornament stuck to my husband's side!"

"Oh, forgive me, dear wife. It's certainly not easy being a beautiful, blond, blue-eyed *gwai lah* in this world! How tragic it must be for you!" Sidney's eyes burned with anger.

"Sidney, my beloved husband—I never claimed it was

easy for you to be an Asian in this imperfect world, but—"

"Pardon me, my old college friends," Tim interrupted. "If I wanted to be involved in a domestic battle, I would not have divorced my sweet wife. I am a busy man. Do you want me to translate this article, or not?"

"Here, Tim. Go ahead and read the goddamned thing," Sid said, abruptly placing the crumpled newspaper into Tim's hands. "What Katie wants, Katie gets."

"Most blonds do get what they want!" Tim laughed as he began to examine the article.

Feeling embarrassed over her argument with Sidney, Katie stared down at the floor, not wishing to make eye contact with either of the men.

"There's something a bit bizarre about a Jew translating an article written in Chinese for a Chinese man and his *gwai lah* wife…" Sidney said with ironic reflection.

Tim laughed as he continued to interpret the article.

"The dead woman's name was See Fong. She was a rather ripe eighty-nine years old when she died in a drowning accident. The authorities speculate she was walking along the Silk River after dark when she lost her footing and fell into the river. And that's that."

Katie responded with a disappointed gaze directed right at Tim.

"What did you expect?" Tim said sarcastically. "Would you have preferred the old woman died from an assassin's gunshot, from a mysterious figure standing on a grassy knoll?"

Sidney pulled at Katie's arm. "There! She's dead by a drowning accident. My sympathy to her family. Now let's go, Katie."

"Not so fast," Katie said. "Tim, you're a brilliant journalist. Answer me this: Why would an eighty-nine-year-old woman be brave enough to walk along a riverbank—alone—after dark? You have a lot of contacts. Can't you do some research on Ms. Fong? Find out anything you can about her, and if there's anyone living who knew her closely? Please, ol' college chum?" Katie gave Tim a reluctant hug as she pleaded.

"All right, I will. But I'd better get a dinner out of this. I'd ask for something more interesting, but Sidney is present," joked Tim.

"Tim, I married a stubborn *gwai lah* bitch," lamented Sidney.

"That must be why we are so compatible," smirked Katie.

The following day, Tim met up with Katie and gave her the information she had requested.

"I managed to obtain some info on the old dead lady. According to the authorities, See Fong has no surviving relatives—at least any they can locate. Her husband, Wu Fong, died in 1975. They had a daughter named Lotus, but she died ages ago in 1933 under some pretty odd circumstances. She was only in her twenties when she dropped dead quite suddenly at a party in Lotus Land. By the way, this Lotus babe was married to a man named Gun Sung. Wasn't Sid's grandfather named Gun Sung?"

"Oh, my God! Sidney never told me Grandpapa Gun was married to another woman before Nana Julie. Please, tell me more!"

Tim continued, "The Lotus stuff was dug up by my girlfriend, who works for the newspaper. And just to let you know, I date her not only because she's one hot babe, but also because she can dig up shit on just about anyone living in China. It seems my girlfriend was working with this ancient fossil of a reporter who knew the Fong family and was even present when the daughter croaked mysteriously. He's retired now. I'll give you his number if you want to talk to him." Tim paused. "Oh, fuck! I almost forgot to add one more rat to the stew. See Fong had a son who died decades ago, as well. My girlfriend, being the snooping cunt she is, looked up some birth records at the courthouse. It appears a Mrs. See Fong gave birth to a son named Lu Fong, but there is no record of her giving birth to a daughter named Lotus."

"What does it mean?" asked Katie, bewildered.

"Fuck if I know," replied Tim. "In a country of over a billion souls, should it be too surprising that some are illegitimate? The old coot could probably give you the answer."

"Tim, if you weren't such an obnoxious dufus, I would sleep with you, but I suppose you at least deserve a hug and a kiss," Katie laughed as she hugged the obese man and pecked him on the cheek.

Katie felt more compelled than ever to paint a clear picture in her thoughts of See Fong. Who was she? And what was her connection to her husband's family?

She massaged her conscious with the pretense that the old woman deserved some identity—some notice of her passing. But in truth, it was a peripheral form of retribution toward her husband's family, who shunned her because of their resentment that Sidney hadn't married within their race. It was for this underlying reason that Katie arranged to meet the old news reporter Tim mentioned. He not only had insightful information about See Fong, but had borne close witness to most of China's turmoil and suffering during the twentieth century.

"Mr. Chew Yuen, such a pleasure to meet one of China's elder statesmen," Katie said gleefully.

"The pleasure is mine to meet such a beautiful *lo fon* from the Gold Mountain," said Chew Yuen. He extended his hand to shake hers as she walked into their prearranged meeting place—a noodle café in the old section of Nanking. The café offered a lovely view of the wide Yangtze River. Odd stares and whispers permeated the dining room as the young, attractive *gwai lah* sat beside the old Chinese man. He was dressed in a traditional dark gray Mao jacket.

"Mr. Chew…" started Katie.

"No, please address me by my *bac goey* name—Jimmy," the old man said as he poured Katie a cup of white tea.

"Jimmy, you now have my undivided attention. Give me something sweet to bite into regarding the old woman See Fong, as well as her daughter Lotus, who expired in 1933." Katie gazed quietly at Jimmy, much like a little girl eagerly waiting for her grandfather to tell her a ghost story.

"As you already know," replied Jimmy, "Lotus was See Fong's daughter. No doubt your in-laws informed you that Lotus was your grandfather-in-law's first wife."

"No! My husband, nor anyone else in the Sung family, never informed me that Grandpa Gun had a first wife named Lotus. Please go on."

"Katie, my pretty *lo fon*, I think first I should fill you in on some things before I tell you about Lotus's death. I knew the Fong family for many years. They were impoverished peasants when I first met them in 1912, the last year of the Ch'ing Dynasty. It was a very troubled time for China after thousands of years of rule by various emperors and empresses. China had now become a republic.

"As I said, the Fongs were poor peasants. They briefly sharecropped land owned by my parents. That year they came to my father to ask for a loan to enable them to finance a journey to China's capital, Peking—now Beijing—to seek better employment. They hoped to drag themselves out of the cesspool of poverty they were mired in. The Forbidden City, a mystic-like dream world of palaces, courtyards and the seat of China's government had great allure to the destitute of China in those days. However, a heavy price was required of those who wished to live and work within those walls, which I will tell you about in a moment.

"My father, being the soft touch that he was, was easily swayed into giving money to anyone with a sob story. He therefore gave the Fong's the money they needed to go to Peking; money the Fong's never repaid my father. At that time the couple had a very bright, handsome boy of four or five years of age.

"As I previously said, 1912 marked the final year of

China's dynastic rule. China was now a republic, but civil servants were still needed to run the affairs of China. The Fongs had aspirations of obtaining some kind of government employment in Peking, until 1912 when Nanking became the nation's capital for a few years. I would not see the Fongs again for eighteen years. In 1930 they returned to Lotus Land, where I was still living at the time. The Fong family that returned home in 1930 was not the same Fong family that left in 1912."

Jimmy paused to slurp down a long strand of noodle, aided by the dexterous use of chopsticks. "The Fongs no longer had a son," he continued, "and in his place was a pretty daughter named Lotus. See Fong informed me that tragically their son Lu had died shortly after their relocation to Peking. He had contracted smallpox, a very common, widespread disease in China at the time. Then, soon after the son's death, See became pregnant with Lotus. Aside from the new daughter and the loss of their son Lu, there was something else that had changed about the Fongs. It seemed to border on complete metamorphosis.

"They had left in dire poverty and returned possessing great wealth. A definite oddity, considering few people in China at that time born to humble beginnings would have any real opportunity to obtain great wealth."

Jimmy paused.

"And what was the Fong's explanation for their newfound riches?" Katie asked as she greedily gulped down the tasty noodles.

"Well," continued Jimmy, "according to See's husband Wu, he worked hard after acquiring a minor civil service job in 1918. He was promoted to a high position within the Forbidden City. Once establishing his fortune, Wu and his family returned to Lotus Land to retire in 1930."

"And you do not believe Mr. Fong's explanation for their much improved financial status?" asked Katie.

"No, no, and no! High civil government positions were

still being held by eunuchs at the time. For centuries eunuchs wielded great power in the emperor's court. Only by becoming a eunuch could a Chinese man, born into poverty, have any opportunity whatsoever to obtain wealth and position. Although the last dynasty ended in 1912, the office of eunuch was not dissolved until 1923. The eunuchs still held several key positions for eleven years after China became a republic. In spite of China's new progressive republic, a young boy was designated a puppet emperor, who became a virtual prisoner behind the walls of the Forbidden City. The eunuchs pulled the strings."

"So, you believe Mr. Fong *did not* make the ultimate sacrifice—a deal with the devil, so to speak? A penis in a pickle jar in exchange for a life of wealth and luxury?" Katie inquired, becoming more engrossed with Jimmy's story.

"Wu Fong left Lotus Land as a man, and returned with all his body parts still attached," Jimmy grinned.

"Of this you are quite certain—you've seen Mr. Fong naked?" Katie asked in subtle jest.

"No! I did not see Mr. Fong naked. I have been married to the same woman for fifty years. And if I were gay, as you *lo fons* say, I would have chosen a man more attractive than Wu Fong," Jimmy said humorously. "But before I give you my reason for knowing Mr. Fong was a rooster and not a hen, I'd like to entertain you with some of these various photos decorating these walls." Jimmy waved a finger toward the numerous faded pictures hanging about the dining room. "Most of these photos were taken by my father before the Communist takeover. Photography was an interesting novelty in those days. My father dearly loved to take photos of anyone who would pose for him. He was very skilled at capturing the souls of his subjects," Jimmy said proudly. "Pay particular attention to this photo of me as a young man."

Jimmy directed Katie's eyes toward a photo of a youthful Chew Yuen embracing an older relative.

"Jimmy, you were such a cute young man. And this

woman you're caressing is very beautiful. I notice a resemblance. I would guess she's either your mother or an aunt," Katie said, smiling at the photo.

The slightly hunched-over Chinese man began to laugh hysterically. "No, no…neither my mother nor an aunt. He is my uncle, Chang Su. The much loved and favored eunuch to Tz'u-his, the last dowager empress of China. Uncle Su left Lotus Land before the turn of the century to seek a high office at the court of Tz'u-his in the Forbidden City. He left a very viral, muscular man, but when he returned, he did not exactly resemble your *gwai lah* movie actor John Wayne. So it's for this reason I knew Wu Fong was still a man of substance—his voice was still baritone and he still sported a goatee!" Jimmy laughed smugly.

"How clever you are, Jimmy. But please, explain in greater detail how Lotus died," said Katie.

"Yes, of course. I remember like it was yesterday. Please notice the photo directly below the one of Uncle Su and me. It's a picture of your grandfather-in-law and Lotus. It was taken at a welcoming party held in honor of their glorious return to Lotus Land. The party was orchestrated by Lotus's parents. Your grandfather-in-law, like the Fongs in 1912, was quite poor. But he had grand dreams to go to the Gold Mountain to seek his fortune, as did thousands of Chinese in the nineteenth and twentieth centuries. Like my father, who financed the Fongs to move to Peking, Wu and See Fong financed Gun Sung's odyssey to the Gold Mountain. And like the merchant of Venice, Gun was required to pay his pound of flesh for the funds he needed to set himself up in America. He was required to marry Lotus and take her to the American dreamland. Now that offers a very paradoxical question: Why would Wu and See force their daughter on a destitute young man when there were so many wealthy young suitors in Lotus Land at the time?" Jimmy raised his hands into the air and shook his head.

"Jimmy, you speak of Grandpa Gun marrying Lotus as if

he was being forced to marry a gay baboon. There are worse things than being forced to marry a young, beautiful woman who comes from a wealthy family." Katie wondered where all this was going.

"Most certainly there are worse fates," continued Jimmy. "But Gun Sung was in love with another woman, a woman he had loved since childhood. Therefore, he was given a choice few men would care to make: Marry a woman he genuinely loved, spending life in dire poverty, or marry someone else, have a loveless marriage and a realistic chance to live atop the Gold Mountain."

"May I venture a guess that Grandpapa's childhood sweetheart was named Julie?" Katie asked, almost rhetorically.

"Yes, so perceptive you are," winked Jimmy. "But of course, you're *gwai lah*—you know everything."

"How lucky for Nana Julie that Lotus would die so untimely," Katie said with a smirk.

"That is very impertinent, my *gwai lah* friend, to imply that Julie Sung had something to do with Lotus's death. I knew Julie from her infancy to when she married Gun Sung and moved to the Gold Mountain with him. She may be bitchy at times, but she could never kill a fellow human," Jimmy said adamantly.

"Oh Jimmy, my new friend—I did not mean to offend you, but sometimes even good people kill given the right circumstances. But let's put Nana Julie aside for the moment. Tell me the scenario of Lotus's death." Katie said carefully, trying to avoid another faux pas.

"Katie, here is the punch line: Lotus died of an overdose of Phenobarbital. Lotus and Gun were having a very jovial time, as was everyone else at the welcome home party. The pair was dancing to *gwai lah* music—a waltz I believe. Once the music ended, the couple sat down at a table. Lotus was laughing hysterically at some humorous story a guest was sharing with everyone at the table. Then suddenly she closed her eyes and slumped forward, her head falling into her bowl of wonton soup.

"According to the autopsy, she died from an overdose of the sedative Phenobarbital. She was addicted to the sedative and apparently took far over the prescribed dosage." Jimmy shrugged his shoulders. "It was ruled an accidental death."

"That's it? How anticlimactic! Is there nothing more? How did the authorities know Lotus was addicted to this sedative?" Katie seemed somewhat disappointed.

"Her husband Gun and her parents all stated that Lotus had this unfortunate addiction to the sedative. My apologies that I could not have told you something more evocative. Death, as well as life, can be so boring," Jimmy said as he refilled Katie's cup with more white tea.

"I assume the authorities tested the food and beverages for various poisons…?" Katie inquired.

"Of course. They found nothing out of the ordinary in the food or drink. Katie, I will make a copy of Lotus's photo for you as a souvenir of what might have been." Jimmy took down the half-century-old photo.

"I would love a copy! May I see the photo once again?" Katie took the photo from Jimmy's hands. "Funny, I didn't notice before that Lotus's cheeks appear swollen. Was she ill? Mumps or some health problem?" Katie scrutinized the photo within a few inches of her eyes.

"Not exactly, unless you call an annoying, rude habit a disease. Though I was quite fond of Lotus, she had this irritating habit of chewing ice cubes which floated about in glasses of your decadent *lo fon* beverage Coca Cola. She did this incessantly.

"Wait! Your curiosity of Lotus's cheeks has awakened my sleeping brain. Shortly before Lotus succumbed to the sedative, she and Gun became very passionate with each other. I remember now, Gun plucked an ice cube from his glass of cola and placed the cube in his mouth. He rolled it about with his tongue, then leaned over and gave Lotus a very sensual, wet kiss. So passionate in fact, that fluid dripped down both their chins. It was a very shocking display of passion considering the conservative nature of Chinese society.

"Shocking, indeed. It would be just another average day if it happened in any Frisco coffee shop!" Katie replied. "Do you remember anything else?"

"Well," Jimmy went on, "one small detail: As the two of them kissed, Gun transferred the ice cube to Lotus's mouth. He then leaped to his feet saying he had an emergency call from nature, and ran off to the bathroom. It was during his absence that one of the guests told the amusing story and Lotus fell dead into her soup."

"Ice cubes from mouth to mouth…how frickin' kinky. Maybe I'll try that with Sidney." Katie smiled at the idea. "Anyway, how is it you would remember Grandpapa Gun going to the bathroom after nearly half a century?"

"It's not so much Gun running to the bathroom that stands out in my mind, but rather the soiling of my best suit!" Jimmy replied with a laugh. "As he jumped up, Lotus's mother, See Fong, shouted to Gun that she'd like another cola when he returned from the bathroom. While she said this, she took the half-filled bottle of Coca Cola and began to pour it into Lotus's glass. In doing this, the idiot caused the glass to fall off the table with its contents decorating my best suit.

"If that wasn't embarrassing enough, the foolish woman then steps on the glass and breaks it while she hurriedly rushed to me to clean my suit with a wet towel." Jimmy rolled his eyes, apparently still agitated after so many years.

"Sorry about your suit, Jimmy," Katie said sympathetically.

"You might also be interested in seeing a photo of Lotus's brother, Lu," Jimmy said as he took another photo off the wall.

Katie closely gazed at the photo of Lotus's brother. She then held up the photo of Lotus and examined it with the same intensity. "Jimmy, please take down the photo of you and Uncle Su. I wish to look at it one last time." Katie took a sip of white tea. A look of deep contemplation was written across her face. She laid the three photos side by side, and rested her chin on the palm of her left hand. "Jimmy, two final questions: Was Nana Julie present at the party? And did your Uncle Su's position as head eunuch make him a wealthy man?" Katie waited in great anticipation for the answers.

"Julie was not present at the party," Jimmy answered. "Why would she be? Lotus married the one man Julie was in love with. But as I've said before, Julie is no killer. She didn't kill Lotus—I believe that strongly.

"As for the answer to your other question, Uncle Su indeed was a very wealthy man as a result of his position as chief eunuch. In fact, many eunuchs became rich. What money they could not gain legally they simply took—all they wanted. The eunuchs had access to the government treasury, the granaries, and government contracts. They awarded them to private companies that greased their palms, and whatever else would make their pockets heavy." Jimmy smiled. "So, my *gwai lah* friend, how have you been enlightened by the information I've given you?"

"Jimmy, my friend, I am constructing a painting from what you've given me. But the painting is not complete. If only I had a few more strokes of paint to add to the canvas." Katie grinned and placed her hand on Jimmy's knee.

"I don't know what picture you're painting, but let me give you one final color," Jimmy said as he took yet another photo off the wall and handed it to her.

"A second photo of your Uncle Su. What is that container your uncle is holding? It appears to be China's well-known ginseng root floating in a jar." She squinted her eyes in puzzlement.

"A root—yes, you could call it that!" Jimmy laughed. "They're actually the objects that separate the men from the eunuchs."

"Oh my God, you can't be serious!" Katie said, her jaw dropping in astonishment.

"I am serious. My dear Uncle Su's sexual organs, preserved in a jar of alcohol," Jimmy replied with a subtle frown.

"But, whatever for?" asked Katie.

"In Chinese society, eunuchs were looked down upon, even though they held high government positions and wealth. Many eunuchs, therefore, tried to hide their missing manhood by adopting children and marrying women in platonic relationships. A man who willingly sacrificed his manhood for material desires would usually be an outcast to his family and denied burial with his ancestors.

"This put the eunuchs in an awkward position. Though I loved Uncle Su dearly, the rest of my family ignored him. Then, when a eunuch died, there was the belief they would be denied eternal life because their body was not perfect— therefore, the spirit was not perfect, either. It is for this reason that most eunuchs paid to have their severed genitals preserved in a jar of alcohol—to thus have their missing parts restored to them in the afterlife."

"Radical! To be buried with your private parts in a pickle jar. It is good we now live in a world where a man does not have to make such a sacrifice to get ahead. Though, unfortunately for we women, we must often grow a penis to get ahead, even now!" Katie giggled.

"So, there you have it. To what purpose all of this will serve you, I don't know, but at least it has given me the opportunity to share noodles and white tea with a beautiful *gwai lah,*" Jimmy said, grasping Katie's hand firmly.

"Indeed," Katie smiled. "All this has given me a chance to dine with a handsome—" Katie stopped in mid-sentence as her eyes bounced rapidly between the three photos. "Jimmy, instead of copies, may I borrow these original photos? I promise you I will return them unharmed."

"You behave as if you've seen an image of the Virgin

Mary in one of the photos," Jimmy remarked. "Please, use them for as long as you wish if you think it will give you peace of mind."

"Thank you. Perhaps I will see you again, good friend." Katie gave the old man a peck on the cheek.

Grabbing those photos, Katie left the noodle café. The sun was setting, bathing the Yangtze in golden light. She leaned against the railing that ran along the river frontage. The cool river breeze felt invigorating after sitting in the stuffy, smoke-filled café. She watched the immense cargo ships pass by slowly. She wrestled with her conscience as to whether she should reveal to her husband and in-laws what she believed to be the truth about Lotus's death long ago—as well as the truth about the death of her mother, See Fong.

I've resented for so long the way Sidney's family has slighted me. But it goes beyond retaliation—there are things that really must be said. Damn the scorn of the Sung family. I care little about them. I can only pray Sidney will still want me after the tempest breaks, Katie thought as she continued to gaze blankly at the immense cargo ships passing by. Tears ran down her face.

―――――――――

"You are one insane bitch, my loving *lo fon* wife," Sidney said as he paced back and forth in their Nanking hotel room. "Why the fuck would you want not only the two of us, but also my parents and Grandmother Julie, to return to Lotus Land?"

"I would not ask this of you or your family if it were not of vital importance. It concerns Lotus, Grandpapa's first wife—which neither you nor anyone else in the Sung family mentioned to me. It also concerns Lotus's mother, See Fong, who died strangely last week." Katie smiled. "What I have to say will enlighten you all!"

"I didn't think my grandfather's first wife was of any importance to you," Sidney said in exasperation.

"She is important to me, and she should be important to your family, as well. My reasons will be explained to you all. If only you all would please return to Lotus Land," pleaded Katie. "That is not a command," Katie added. "I am only a *gwai lah* woman, I am only asking politely." She grasped Sidney's hands and gave them a gentle kiss. "I will wait four days for you and your family at the public hall in Lotus Land where your grandfather's funeral reception was held. I will sit obediently for your arrival from 3:00 p.m. to 5:00 p.m." Katie still held Sidney's hands tightly, waiting for a reply.

"And if my family and I shouldn't arrive…then what?" asked Sidney.

"Then I can only hope that I will still have a husband who I love very much. In any case, I would then grow old and eventually die without revealing a story that I believe needs to be told. I now leave for Lotus Land," Katie said. She kissed her husband and held him tightly, then grabbed her luggage and left to catch the train.

Once arriving in Lotus Land, Katie checked into the same hotel she and Sidney had stayed in only a few days earlier. Once she was settled, she walked the few blocks to the public hall, carrying with her a thickly wrapped package and the three photos she had borrowed from Jimmy.

She sat alone in the rather austere building. The stench from the human excrement and the damp hot air seemed even more oppressive than it had a few days earlier. She sipped bottled water she'd brought with her, and incessantly and nervously checked her wristwatch, even though a large clock hung on the wall facing her.

As promised, Katie would wait for them until 5:00 p.m., when the clock in the town square began its morose ringing and she realized her husband and his family weren't coming. She would then gather her package and photos and leave the hall by the clock's fifth ring. Katie carried out this sullen routine for the next three days. By the fourth and final day, Katie had grown very despondent sitting alone once again in the drab hall. The two hours passed with an agonizing slowness.

What can I do but return to the Gold Mountain and face Sidney and his aloof family, thought Katie. *If I can never speak my mind, the ghosts of Lotus and See will haunt me forever.*

As the clock began to routinely resonate its five rings announcing the five o'clock hour, the blond *lo fon* woman began to walk out of the hall dejectedly for the last time.

"My apologies, my cherished wife," called a remorseful Sidney as Katie opened the front door. He and the other Sung family members stood at the entrance. "Katie, excuse the lateness, but as you might have guessed, it took a great deal of coaxing to get my family to return to Lotus Land."

"The audacity of *gwai lahs!* You'd better have something quite evocative to say to us, young lady," Grandmother Julie said, clearly agitated.

"Daughter-in-law, quickly come to the point," said an equally agitated Grace, Katie's mother-in-law. "If you wish to divorce Sidney, this could have waited until we returned to the Gold Mountain."

"No, I'm not divorcing Sidney. But he may wish to divorce me after I inform you all what I believe to be true. This is a chance I must take." Katie was determined. "Please, let us sit together." Katie pointed to the very same table they had sat at during Gun's funeral reception.

While they seated themselves, Katie placed the mysteriously wrapped package in the center of the table. She then placed the three framed photos, stacked atop each other, on the table in front of her.

"Nana Julie, please look at this first photo," Katie said, handing the photo to her grandmother-in-law.

"A picture of Lotus! How did you obtain this photo?" Julie demanded. "How did you learn of my husband's first wife?"

"The explanation is too lengthy and irrelevant. The point is, I know who Lotus is. Now allow me to refresh all of you with some long-forgotten memories. The year was 1933, a very prosperous Gun and Lotus Sung return to China, the land of their birth—return to Lotus Land, to be more specific. They returned after three fruitful years on the Gold Mountain. A homecoming party was held in their honor. Tragically, Lotus dies under bizarre circumstances while at the party," Katie explained.

"A sedative overdose, no more, no less," Burt Sung, Katie's father-in-law, finally spoke out. "You disappoint me, my daughter-in-law. You've told us nothing that is not public record."

Katie went on, "And is it public record that Lotus was murdered? And were you also aware that her mother, See Fong, who died only last week, was also possibly murdered?" Katie's eyes danced from one Sung family member to another as she spoke with a smug confidence in her beliefs.

"Impertinent bitch," Grace said. "You can't seriously believe what you've just said!"

"And who is the fictitious person or persons responsible for these murders you fantasize about?" Burt asked.

"Grandpapa Gun, I regret to say, took the life of Lotus," said Katie in a solemn, apologetic voice.

"Preposterous garbage! How can you dishonor our beloved father in such a manner?" Burt said, greatly offended.

"I may be a silly *lo fon* bitch, but I believe that this time I am correct. First, I must backtrack and give a prologue as to the situations that led up to this horrid crime. In 1912, there was an impoverished couple named Wu and See Fong. They lived in Lotus Land with their sweet little son, perhaps four or five years of age, named Lu. In that year, the family left Lotus Land to seek a better life in Peking. Leaping forward to 1930, the couple then returned to Lotus Land with a great deal of money, minus their son Lu who, according to the mother, unfortunately died of smallpox, a common health problem in China at the time. In place of the young son, the couple returned with a beautiful young daughter, who was born to them soon after their move to Peking." Katie's voice intensified as she spoke.

"What an insightful revelation, my darling daughter-in-law," said Burt. "But you've said nothing we don't already know."

"*Lo fons* are notorious for speaking a great deal but saying very little," Grace added rudely.

"Allow Katie to finish," Sidney interjected. "We've come this far, why not let my wife speak her mind?"

"Yes, let the silly *lo fon* bitch talk," Julie said, attempting to lighten the moment.

Katie could not resist a slight chuckle at Nana Julie's remark.

"All right, what I have to say next is so incredulous that it could not possibly be real—but I believe it to be true," Katie said. "First, I wish to pass these two photos around. There is one of Lu Fong as a young boy, and the other of his sister as a young woman, taken on the day of her death."

The Sung family passed the photos around, each of them examining them indifferently.

"I see two photos," Grace said. "One of a young boy, the other picture is of his sister Lotus. The young boy is sitting on the lap of some well-dressed, young Chinese man. I see nothing else."

"The young man holding the boy in his lap has a glass in one hand, perhaps a soft drink," added Sidney. "But I see nothing peculiar or out of place in either photo."

"Try this: The two photos of brother and sister are fiction. There was no brother and sister named Lu and Lotus," Katie said enigmatically.

"What are you saying, dear wife?" Sidney asked, confused. "I see a photo of a boy and a young woman, supposedly they are brother and sister. If not, who are they? There is a strong resemblance between them."

"Of course they resemble each other. Why shouldn't they...*when it's two photos of the same person!* Taken perhaps twenty years apart, but the same person, nonetheless." Katie grinned with the feeling of one-upmanship.

"You are quite insane!" Julie said, giving Katie a glare. "I would not be surprised if you also hear voices!"

"Any voices I hear are from Lotus and her mother See, asking for their souls to be set free by the truth. To state it plainly, Lotus was in fact a man—a eunuch pretending to be a woman. Because Lu—or Lotus, I should say—was physically attractive with delicate features, he could easily pass for a woman." Katie held up the two photos to further emphasize her point.

The Sungs burst into uproarious laughter.

"Bullshit!" screamed Burt. "I believe that is the term you *lo fons* use so freely when someone is lying."

"Please Burt, let's not be insulting," Grace said, struggling to contain her laughter. "Katie is our son's wife."

"All right then," continued Burt. "I will humor our daughter-in-law by asking how she knows Lu and Lotus are one and the same. Well, Katie?"

"I will pass these photos around once again. Please notice there's a cute little birthmark on the young boy's right cheek. Coincidentally, there is also an identical cute little birthmark on Lotus's right cheek," Katie offered. "But there's something else that seems oddly coincidental. There is a dear old man named Chew Yuen who I recently became acquainted with. He knew the Fong family well—before they left Lotus Land and after they returned. The old Chinese gentleman told me that Lotus had the annoying habit of chewing ice cubes and was particularly fond of iced Coca Colas. Now, if you will please notice how puffy Lotus's cheeks are. The reason is that her mouth is full of ice. By the way, the young Chinese man holding Lu is Mr. Chew Yuen, who I spoke about," explained Katie as she pointed to the figures in the photos.

"Dear wife, all you have is a cute little mole on the cheek of a brother and his sister, and as you've pointed out, the two siblings both enjoyed chewing ice!" Sidney remarked.

"No I have more. I did my homework," Katie said smugly. "There is no birth record of a Lotus Fong in Peking during that period."

"It proves nothing," Grace argued. "China in that era, including any time in China up to the present, has been very turbulent. It is not surprising that the government officials kept poor records of China's people."

"Putting aside the idiotic facts you've accumulated, how dare you imply that my father was a homosexual?" shouted Burt. "In fact, my father had numerous affairs with both *lo fon* and *hong en*—Chinese—women. There is no way in goddamn hell that my father could have been gay!"

"Thank you for informing the world about my husband's many adulterous affairs," Julie replied sarcastically.

"My deepest apologies, Mother. I—"

Katie interrupted. "I did not say or imply Grandpapa Gun was a homosexual, but he married Lu, or Lotus, if you will, for a very strong ulterior motive. This is what I believe occurred. It is a rather twisted and complicated story.

"As you may already be aware, eunuchs were shunned and looked down upon by most people in China. Even their families shunned them, in much the same fashion you all have treated me since I married Sidney three years ago." Katie spoke with a strong, heated voice to get her point across.

Sidney's parents and grandmother looked away from Katie and Sidney in shock and embarrassment after hearing Katie's biting remarks.

"Stop eyeing the floor and look at me!" Katie demanded. "As I was saying, eunuchs were looked down upon by most people. Some in fact adopted children and then passed them off as their own. They'd then marry a woman in a platonic relationship. But these poor souls would have difficulty getting away with the ruse, because the eunuch's voice would become higher and they would take on a more feminine appearance. To compensate for the eunuchs becoming outcasts, most of them, if not all, gained a great amount of wealth siphoning off great sums of government money, having had access to the government treasury, allocating government contracts, and any other means of taking government and royal money. This draws me to a theory I have: If a eunuch could not always get away with a make-believe wife and family, perhaps the eunuch would have another alternative. He could pretend to be a woman—not an overly difficult task considering the eunuch no longer had the attributes of a man. But of course, the family would still be aware that their newfound daughter, granddaughter, niece or whatever, was once a son, grandson, or nephew. Armed with this knowledge, the family would still secretly feel great shame for their changed male relative. So, why not deaden the pain and humiliation for both the family and the lost son by having him-her move away...far, far away. Far away as a place called the Gold Mountain—America!" Katie drew a breath and continued. "But it would be much to conspicuous for a eunuch posing as a woman to go to the Gold Mountain alone. He-she would need a husband, and this is where Grandpapa Gun comes into play. The family and/or Lotus chose Grandpapa Gun to be the future husband—to be Lotus's protector, companion, and most important, Lotus's cover. Why Gun? Because he was poor. A rich man would simply not do. If the man were already rich, he would have little desire to pull up roots and seek a new life in an alien world. Undoubtedly, Lotus's parents paid Grandpapa Gun handsomely to marry Lotus and take him-her to live in America.

"It would have made little difference if Gun knew beforehand that Lotus was not the pretty female he-she appeared to be. Grandpapa Gun was desperate; he needed funds to make it to a place where the streets were paved with gold and money grew on trees. Other than becoming a eunuch himself, Gun had little or no chance whatsoever of becoming successful if he remained in China. And as you are all aware, Grandpapa Gun became a great success after immigrating to the Gold Mountain."

"You're speculating. Fantasy, pure and simple," Julie responded to Katie's theory.

"Do you have any proof Lu Fong lived into adulthood, became a eunuch, and then took on this ludicrous façade as a woman?" Burt asked.

"Regrettably, there is no record of a Lu Fong being a civil servant eunuch during that era. But certainly, if a man can pretend to be a woman, it shouldn't be too much of a surprise that he could also change his name," Katie said in defense.

"Let's say that you are correct," Grace said with great offense toward Katie's assumptions. "That Lu Fong was a eunuch pretending to be a woman, and my father-in-law was desperate enough—or stupid enough—to marry a castrated man. That would not prove that my father-in-law was a killer."

"My apologies, Grace, but I believe Gun did slay Lotus, with Wu and See Fong as his co-conspirators." Katie's eyes widened and her lips tightened in defiance.

"Then I am certain my clever *gwai lah* daughter-in-law will inform us of the how and why," Grace said, looking around the room with a slight smile of disbelief.

"I would be happy to," Katie smirked. "It was a near perfect plan. You have a son who the parents are ashamed of, and you have a man who is married to a man, pretending to be a woman. Might I add that this man, Gun, was deeply in love with you, Nana Julie. Both Gun and Lotus sold their souls for material values. A rather poor exchange, if you ask me. But in any case, Wu and See's unwanted son—or daughter—was now out of sight and out of mind, thousands of miles away in a brave new world. Wu and See Fung were free to spend their son's ill-gotten booty as they wished, and the people of Lotus Land would never know their hideous secret. But who would have guessed—certainly not Wu and

See Fong—that the prodigal son-daughter would one day return to China.

"Gun and Lotus's reason for returning to Lotus Land would only be speculation on my part, but I think I would be hitting close to home if I said Gun returned to see his true love, Julie, once again. And maybe Lotus's reason for returning was to spite his-her parents, and to flaunt their new high status as Chinese Americans. It is for these reasons, or something close, that possessed Gun and Lotus to return home to China. But regardless of the reason, Lotus was like a pesky fly that would not stop buzzing around the heads of his parents and husband. If Lotus were to reveal to the citizenry of Lotus Land his true sexual identity, his parents would no doubt be embarrassed beyond words—and even more so for Grandpapa Gun. And we can't overlook Gun's love for you, Nana Julie. Most certainly Grandpapa Gun and Lotus's parents were more than eager to swat that annoying fly."

Katie paused.

"More bullshit!" Burt exclaimed, gritting his teeth.

"Please Burt, let me finish," Katie said. "I told you why, now I'll explain how. Lotus was poisoned, and that I'm sure of."

"Nonsense," stated Julie. "No poison was found in any of the food or drink that was served the day of the party. The authorities even said that."

"Correct you are, and Lotus had an addiction to Phenobarbital, or so Lotus's parents and the husband said. But this is how I think Lotus actually died. My theory is far more insidious.

"As I stated, Lotus had a nervous habit of chewing ice cubes, and unfortunately that was her sad undoing. Chew Yuen, or Jimmy as his close friends call him, was present at the homecoming party. He related to me something very curious that happened to Lotus only moments before her sudden death: In an atypical display of open affection, Gun sat on Lotus's lap, and in a festive and amorous mood, he plucked an ice cube from Lotus's glass of Coca Cola and placed it in his mouth. He rolled it around a bit with his tongue, then he proceeded to give Lotus a rather passionate, wet kiss, erotically transferring the ice cube from his mouth to Lotus's. Lotus of course, having a penchant for chewing ice cubes, gladly accepted and began chewing it. What Lotus was not aware of was that Gun had placed a large dose of Phenobarbital in his mouth shortly before placing the ice cube in his mouth. Phenobarbital, by the way, is odorless and tasteless." Katie paused. Her listeners clung intently to every word. "Grandpapa Gun must have placed the sedative in his mouth by pretending to wipe it with a napkin, or being at a fun party, he might have slipped the substance into his mouth while the others were distracted by the loud music or an amusing anecdote being told by one of the guests. He then hurriedly ran to the bathroom under the pretense he had eaten something that didn't agree with him. But in truth, he did so to quickly rinse out his mouth so that he, too, wouldn't become ill or succumb to the sedative. In the meantime, dear Lotus unknowingly swallows the sedative overdose along with the ice, and thereby ruins a perfectly good bowl of wonton soup. And that," Katie finished with a subtle smile of confidence, "is that."

"Pure madness!" Julie said. "How can you be certain that what you're saying is the actual manner in which Lotus died?"

"There are no sure things in life other than death, but I have candidly told you what I believe to be how and why Lotus died. But placing her aside for a moment, I also believe See Fong was murdered."

"More lies on top of lies! You disgust me!" Julie yelled, standing abruptly and slapping the table to further emphasize her disdain.

"Julie, allow me to point something out that I have never told anyone before. The night of See Fong's death, I saw you leave the hotel we were staying in. You left shortly after dark and returned a few hours later. You were perspiring and seemed very distraught over something. At the time I thought nothing of your odd behavior—until I read about See Fong's death in the newspaper. Then I put it all together. It makes one wonder—why would a woman your age be out alone at that time of night? And why were you so upset? Did you kill somebody?" Katie added snidely.

Tears began to stream down the old woman's face.

"Beloved wife," Sidney said in a harsh voice, "do not malign my grandmother! Have you no human decency?"

"I happen to have plenty of decency, but I would ask the same question of your family."

"Katie, rather than continue with this serve-and-volley of criticism," challenged Burt, "let me say this: All of your surreal claims rest on one premise, and that is that Lotus and Lu Fong were one and the same person. You have no solid proof that Lotus was in fact a castrated man."

"As a matter of fact, I do have proof beyond a shadow of a doubt," Katie replied. "I offer you this third photo. It is a photo of a eunuch. It is Chew Yuen's uncle, and in this photo he is holding a laboratory specimen jar. And the jar contains the poor man's genitals. Quite commonly eunuchs had their private parts preserved and buried with them so they could be whole again in the afterlife—and thus regain the respect they'd lost in their previous life," explained Katie.

"And this small historical fact proves what?" asked Grace.

"Please," Katie continued, "bear with me. I have ample proof in this package."

Katie cut the string that bound the wrappings on her enigmatic package. She quickly pulled away the wrappings, then revealed a thick glass specimen jar with indescribable objects floating about.

"What is this, a joke?" Grace asked, bewildered.

"No, it's the family jewels of Lotus—or Lu Fong Sung, if you will. It was taken from the coffin that held the body of Lotus Fong." Katie jiggled the jar, causing the objects to swim about.

"Nonsense! How could a *gwai lah*, a woman *gwai lah* at that, possibly obtain a court-ordered permit to exhume Lotus's body?" Burt asked with surprise.

"I never said anything about a permit, I simply bribed two cemetery groundskeepers to dig up the body and remove the jar of goodies," answered Katie.

"What a vile, obscene person you are, Katie! To desecrate a man's final resting place would be quite unethical in any culture!" Julie shouted.

"I beg your pardon...did you say desecrate a *man's* grave? Supposedly, Lotus was a woman, remember?" Katie smiled with amusement at having caught her grandmother-in-law in a mistake of words.

"Bitch! That's the second time you've insulted my mother!" screamed Burt.

"Enough!" Julie cried. "Enough! Katie is correct about nearly everything! It is true my husband Gun killed Lotus, and yes—Lotus was a man, as well as a eunuch! Gun and I loved each other very much. It was the only way for us to be together. Wu and See had heartily agreed to conspire to kill their disgraced son. See pretended to accidentally break Lotus's soft drink glass in case Lotus drank from it after Gun put the sedative in Lotus's mouth, which may have placed some of the residue on the glass."

The room was silent as everyone stared at the old woman with amazement at her confession.

Julie continued, "You have no idea how repulsive my husband felt when he kissed Lotus, not only because he was a man, but because he was an arrogant, obnoxious human being. For years we kept this secret. Gun and I were forced to pay Wu and See Fong for what seemed an eternity to keep them silent."

"This would not have been necessary if the idiots had not squandered Lotus's fortune on frivolous things and lavish parties," said Katie.

"But one item you are incorrect about, my brilliant

granddaughter-in-law: See Fong died by accident. She had demanded that we meet along the river after dark. As usual, she wanted more money. While standing on the high riverbank, she lost her footing and fell in. She screamed for help as she struggled in the swift water, but I am an old woman, and the bank was steep. How could I have saved her? I could do nothing but watch the cold water eventually consume See. I then walked back to the hotel. It was all quite sad to watch See die the way she did, but as I said, there was nothing I could have done." Julie paused, then went on, "I am sorry. I apologize to all of you, but especially to you, Katie. I am sorry not only for the crime my husband committed long ago, but also for behaving so coldly to you after you married Sidney. It's only natural that grandmothers would want their grandchildren to marry within their race—but I think Sidney made a good choice." She held Katie's hands firmly and cried.

"What a foul kettle of fish my family has cooked for our descendants," Sid finally said remorsefully.

"Katie, why have you gone through so much trouble to discover my father's indiscretions?" asked Burt.

"To mock and shame us!" said Grace.

"Not at all!" Katie replied. "I suppose I did it to set Lu and See's souls free. No, not precisely—I did it to prove to all of you that I am a person of value. If anyone has been mocked or shamed, it would be me—by all of you!" Katie finished in a scolding voice.

"We apologize," said Grace. "I congratulate you on your determination and strong will. Do you plan to take this knowledge to the Chinese authorities?"

"No. What would be the point? Grandpapa Gun is dead. He now faces a higher authority than the Chinese justice system. I will let sleeping dogs lie. To awaken them would only let them bite us on our asses."

"You have more strength and substance that I gave you credit for. Welcome to the Sung family," said Julie as she caressed her Katie.

"I also welcome you to the family," Burt said. He and Grace took turns hugging Katie.

"See you back on the Gold Mountain," said Julie as she, Burt, and Grace left the hall.

Sidney turned to Katie. "Katie, my wife, I know your motives for doing this were quite sincere, but nonetheless, your theft of Lu's genitals was most cruel and irreverent. I'm just not sure I can forgive you." He gazed down at the floor as he spoke.

"What makes you think I would desecrate a person's remains?" Katie laughed. "You and your family actually believed you were looking at Mr. Winkie and his associates? What you're looking at is a white asparagus stalk and two peeled turnips floating in alcohol." Katie bent over with laughter.

"My outrageous, clever wife! Wait until my parents and Grandmother Julie hear about this!" Sidney said, joining his wife in laughter.

"Yes, and what a lovely bedtime story it will make for our soon-to-be first child," said Katie with a twinkle in her eye.

"Our what?" exclaimed Sidney.

— The End —

The Last Chinaman

His name was Tang Wing, and like most Chinese immigrants he had changed his first name to a Christian name, James, after James Madison, the fourth president of the United States. He was my Uncle Jimmy, but for the first thirty-five years of my life I knew him only through the dim recollections of my father, aunts and other uncles, and a single yellowed photograph of Jimmy and his bride on their wedding day. As I grew into adulthood, I gradually forgot Uncle Jimmy, just as one forgets a favorite hat that is discarded when it has become frayed and worn. Who would have guessed that the hat would someday return, still frayed and worn?

It was the usual sweltering-hot day in the Sacramento Valley that summer in 1985. Known as Twin Bluffs, this was the town of my birth. I remember hearing the sound of a decrepit '56 Ford pickup truck pulling up the driveway to my home, its motor groaning like a dying cow. Out of the truck stepped an elderly Chinese man in his early seventies. His face looked like cracked leather that had been sitting in the sun for too many years; however, the sparkle in his eyes and the quickness of his steps belied his age.

My initial impression of this man was that he must be some dirty, vagabond Chinaman who had seen my family name written in Chinese on the carport and decided to ask for a handout. Instead, he extended his hand. With tears in his eyes he said, "Goddamn it, *I Goo*. I'm finally home!"

Hearing *I Goo*, which means "big brother" in my native tongue, surprised me. As I gazed at this odd old man, the memories of my father's brash *sigh law*, or kid brother, who left his family some fifty years ago for places and dreams unknown, came racing back.

In a state of shock I accepted his hand and blurted, "Are you my Uncle Jimmy?"

As if he didn't hear me, or simply chose not to, he said, "*I Goo,* goddamn it, don't you recognize me? It's me, Jimmy. Was it '35 or '36 when I left? You haven't changed a minute, *I Goo.*"

"Uncle Jimmy," I responded. "I am not your brother George. My father died in 1970. I am his son, George, Jr."

Jimmy ignored me and ranted on about how young I still looked after all these years. After pleading with him, trying to convince him that I was his nephew and not his brother George, I finally gave up. "You crazy old man," I said. "You believe what you want to believe."

I suppose he was like many people who do not want to face reality and grow old gracefully, but he seemed to take it a step further, refusing to accept that he'd grown old at all. My newfound uncle was clearly not dealing with a full deck and was definitely in need of a good meal and a bath. The reeking odor of cheap wine and cheap cigars didn't exactly curry favor with the nephew he had never known.

"*I Goo,* I'm so sorry for my failings. Can you ever forgive me?" he asked.

I didn't answer him. Instead, I ushered him into the house rather quickly so my neighbors wouldn't see my unsightly relative.

While Uncle Jimmy bathed, I prepared an old family recipe of steamed fish in black bean sauce over rice. I reflected about what my father and other relatives had told me about Uncle Jimmy when I was growing up. It seemed he had always been a hell-raiser, constantly getting into trouble with the law. He stole cars and went for joyrides, making frequent visits to the Jade Palace in Twin Bluffs' Chinatown, which ran along the river. My grandmother called the residents of the Jade Palace "working ladies," but Herbie

Chew, who had been my best friend throughout grammar school, told me that a more accurate title was "whore."

Uncle Jimmy was an atypical Chinaman in those days. Back then most Chinese kept a low profile. The very fact that Caucasians, or *lo fons* as we called them, segregated the Chinese to their own separate sections of American cities (Chinatowns) made us realize all too well that we were different. I suppose Uncle Jimmy's rebelliousness was his way of expressing defiance in an imperfect world. He always said that he didn't mind the *lo fons* calling him "Chinaman," though it was considered a derogatory term by most Chinese. After all, how could one word represent all the pain and humiliation the Chinese have had to put up with over the years from the *low fons?*

My father, George Sr., always thought his kid brother was a spoiled brat. My grandmother was nearly fifty when Jimmy was born. He was her ninth and last child. Because he was more like a grandchild than a son, my grandmother doted on him, lavishing far more affection on Uncle Jimmy than any of her other eight children. At that time, my grandparents were quite prosperous. Their parents before them came to California during the Gold Rush in 1850 to seek the American Dream, and the family had a successful business. It seemed such a paradox that, years later, one of the family would become a homeless bum. I myself was a grocery clerk making only seven dollars an hour.

After a hot bath and a meal that Uncle Jimmy practically inhaled, we sat on lawn chairs in my backyard. Over a couple of beers I asked the one question I was most curious about: "Why did you return to Twin Bluffs after so many years?"

"Oh," he said casually, "I'm going to die in a few weeks, perhaps a few months, and I wanted to visit my roots and say goodbye."

I wasn't sure if he was serious. "Jimmy, what kind of shit is this? You can't be serious. Are you ill?"

"*I Goo,* you never take me seriously! Goddamn it! Of

course I'm really dying. You think I'd come home after fifty years just to bullshit you? A doctor in New Orleans told me that I have advanced lung cancer. But no matter! What the hell! I've been everywhere and done everything. I only regret having let you and the rest of the family down, especially Lotus."

After the shock of hearing Uncle Jimmy's words I apologized for not believing him. It seemed rather sad that the uncle I'd only known for a few hours would be leaving as quickly as he had arrived. It was hard to fathom that the sum total of a man's life was measured by endless bottles of cheap liquor, loose women, and traveling a road that led nowhere— and then dying alone.

"Jimmy, I think you should think about getting your affairs in order," I suggested.

"What goddamn affairs? I have nothing except this old '56 Ford truck. I will give it to you, *I Goo!*"

I thanked him for such a generous gift, which I would no doubt have to haul away when I took possession of it.

"*I Goo,* you were right. I never was any good. I didn't deserve a fine woman like Lotus. Please, take me to her grave. Later we can visit all of our brothers and sisters."

I didn't have the heart to tell him that all three of his brothers and three of his five sisters were dead. So, I told him that all of our remaining relatives had moved away. Most of the Chinese community had left Twin Bluffs when so many *lo fons* moved into Madrona County, taking all of the best paying jobs. The Chinese moved down into San Francisco, or *eye fowl,* "the big city." I explained to Uncle Jimmy that I was the only Chinaman dumb enough to stay, which was the truth. "I'm the last Chinaman, Jimmy," I said.

Though there was no longer any family other than myself to greet him in Twin Bluffs, I thought I could at least take him to the family plot at the Blue Oak Cemetery to see the grave of his bride, Lotus. When Jimmy mentioned Lotus it brought back a flood of memories. My family had told many stories about the beautiful young bride brought to America in an arranged marriage. She was a fiery, strong-willed young woman of sixteen who arrived in America to tame the heart of a brash young Chinese man who was out of control.

To show atonement for his past behavior, Jimmy had consented to marry Lotus. They seemed like an odd couple, always arguing. Lotus complained that she had been purchased like an expensive tin of tea, and Uncle Jimmy complained about how he'd lost his freedom and that he had had far more beautiful women than Lotus. But deep down there was a genuine love for one another, and for the first time in Uncle Jimmy's life he felt a real closeness and purpose in his life. Perhaps he never felt he belonged to the white man's world, or to my grandparents' world, and Lotus gave him that feeling of belonging.

It brought great joy to the whole family when Lotus announced that she was expecting a child. Impending fatherhood would bind Uncle Jimmy even closer to Lotus. As with many ancient cultures, a boy child would be highly prized by the entire family. He would carry on the family name and take care of his parents in their old age, whereas a girl child would only be tolerated and considered just another mouth to feed. It was with this thought in mind that Lotus promised the family a boy.

As Lotus grew bigger with child, the family doted on her and taught her the customs to be carried out once the child was born. Uncle Jimmy worked for the first time in his life, running the family's general goods store in Chinatown. My grandmother, who was an amateur palm reader, foretold that Lotus and Jimmy would have many sons, be very rich, and live long lives. It seemed to be a promising future, but my grandmother foretold the same future in every palm she read. Unfortunately, Lotus and Uncle Jimmy's destiny would prove to be far more grotesque than my grandmother predicted.

Late one night during the seventh month of her pregnancy Lotus began to hemorrhage. Uncle Jimmy called

Dr. Westerman and begged him to come.

"You goddamn Chinaman! How dare you call me at this hour!" Dr. Westerman growled. "Give her two aspirin and bring her to my office in the morning."

Uncle Jimmy, my aunts, and my grandmother sat up with Lotus throughout the night. As the sun rose over the valley, Lotus whispered to Uncle Jimmy, "Take care of my crimson-fleshed peach tree and take care of yourself, my beloved Jimmy."

And with that, Lotus took her last breath and closed her eyes for good.

Jimmy ran to the closet and grabbed his hunting rifle, intending to kill Dr. Westerman. My father pulled the rifle away from him and knocked him down.

"You damn fool! Lotus was the only thing that gave your life meaning, and now you would dishonor her by taking a *lo fon's* life? It won't bring her back."

Without saying a word Uncle Jimmy rose to his feet, walked out the front door, and drove away in the brand new Packard, a wedding gift from my grandparents.

It would be three months before the family would hear from Uncle Jimmy. He sent a postcard from Havana, Cuba, which read: *The past grows too heavy for us all. Please forgive my shortcomings.* The next postcard would not come for two decades. Postmarked Los Angeles, 1955, it read: *Am breaking into the movies. Have met John Wayne, Gary Cooper and Humphrey Bogart. Love always, Jimmy. P.S. I am the cultural consultant for John Wayne's new movie,* Blood Alley. Years later my father found out from a friend who lived in Hollywood that Uncle Jimmy had been no more than a flunky who moved props around the movie sets.

It wasn't until that hot summer afternoon in 1985 that I alone, the last family member living in Twin Bluffs, would see Jimmy again. Most of what he had done, the people he had met, and the places he had been for the last half century would go with him to his grave.

As the hours of that hot afternoon wore on, Uncle Jimmy and I talked mostly about our family history, good times and bad. We discussed how Grandfather Woo came to America during the Gold Rush to seek his fortune, and how he, like so many Chinese, was forced to face reality and take work piling heavy rocks, one on top of the other, for ten cents a day. He and others like him built the rock walls that now stretch throughout the foothills of the Sacramento Valley, like an endless serpent from a Chinese folktale. We also recalled how Grandfather Woo saved for ten years to bring my great grandmother to America. Somewhere along the way it seemed that the American Dream had become a nightmare. The Chinese name for America was *Gim Sam,* meaning "Gold Mountain." Sadly, most would realize the Gold Mountain was really nothing but a mountain of cheap volcanic rock that passed through the hands of thousands of immigrants who bled, suffered, and died over them.

"Yes, *I Goo,* I saw those endless rock walls as I drove into town. They stretch from the Sacramento River into the foothills," Uncle Jimmy said. "They appear the same today as they did fifty years ago."

Uncle Jimmy then brought up the crimson-fleshed peach tree, brought to America as a young sapling by Lotus. It was a rare variety of peach that few people grew any longer. Its popularity, like a lot of things in life, just faded away.

"Uncle Jimmy, Chinatown no longer exists in Twin Bluffs," I told him. "It has all been replaced by county buildings, law offices, and yogurt shops. I'm sorry to say that the County Records and Supplies building now stands where your home once did. In 1968 our family, along with many others, was forced to sell our home to the county at half the fair market price to make way for new development."

"*I Goo,* let's go see. The tree may still be standing."

I doubted the tree would still be there, but I decided to humor my newfound uncle and we went to find the spot where his house once stood.

As we approached the Madrona County Building of Records and Supplies, Uncle Jimmy shouted, "Holy shit! Look, *I Goo*, there it is! Lotus's peach tree!"

Off the south side of the building was a small courtyard where Lotus's peach tree stood, bearing a single peach. As we drove closer, Uncle Jimmy suddenly jumped out of my car, ran to the tree and plucked the peach from the branch. As he ran back to the car a county employee ran out of the building and chased after Jimmy, cursing at the old Chinaman for stealing county property. I couldn't help but laugh at the absurdity of the entire scene as we sped away to the Blue Oak Cemetery.

In a grave sandwiched between my paternal grandmother and my cousin Julia was Lotus, who had died in 1935 at the age of eighteen. I waited by the car while Uncle Jimmy visited the grave. He took the peach out of his soiled woolen coat and cut it in half. He placed one-half near Lotus's headstone, then ate the other half. He spoke for a few minutes to the headstone, then kissed it and turned and walked back to the car. As he approached, I wondered what twists and turns he had made throughout his life, and thought how sad it was for him to return home after fifty years to be greeted only by a nephew who hadn't even been born yet when he left.

As Uncle Jimmy opened my car door to get in, he suddenly fell over backwards and began coughing violently and spitting up blood. I rushed him to the hospital, where he underwent emergency surgery. For the next few days he faded in and out of consciousness; however, during his waking hours he was quite lucid.

"*I Goo*, I'm sorry for letting you and everyone else down," he said.

"That's all water under the bridge now, *sigh law*," I said. "The important thing now is that you're home."

I felt such pity for the old man. If only he had realized that when he ran away to escape his unbearable sorrow, he could not run away from himself—that he had to accept his past, which couldn't be undone, and get on with his life.

Six days after his emergency operation I received an incredible phone call at 3:00 a.m. from the hospital. Uncle Jimmy had escaped from his room, barefoot, wearing nothing but his hospital gown. At daybreak the police found him walking alongside the freeway. It took four officers to subdue the seventy-two-year-old man who was dying of cancer. As they drove him back to the hospital, he kept ranting about how he wanted to pick a crimson-fleshed peach for his wife Lotus.

Less than twenty-four hours later Uncle Jimmy was dead. He died in his sleep. I buried him next to Lotus. There was no funeral, and I alone watched as my father's long-forgotten kid brother was lowered into the ground. Three months later I quit my job as a grocery clerk at Sonny's Supermarket and, like so many Chinese before me, left Twin Bluffs to seek a better paying job in the eye fowl.

The following summer I visited the family plot in Twin Bluffs, bringing the customary fruits and coins sealed in red envelopes. Lotus's peach tree had been cut down several months earlier to make way for a statue of President Reagan. I couldn't find a crimson-fleshed peach anywhere else, and hoped the common freestone peaches I brought would be enough for Jimmy and Lotus.

As I placed the peaches beside their graves, I noticed something scribbled on Uncle Jimmy's headstone: *Here lies Twin Bluffs' last Chinaman.*

— The End —

Ella Sue's Bird's Nest Soup

The young couple entering a Chinese restaurant on Grant Avenue in San Francisco's Chinatown drew the attention of everyone in the room. Both man and woman were tall, sporting wide brimmed cowboy hats, and wore custom-made ostrich leather boots on their feet.

"Hey, yella part'ner, bring me a thick rib-eye steak, an make it so rare it's still mooing," said the man with an irritating chuckle.

The thirty-something Chinese waiter, Willie Chew, rolled his eyes. "Um, sir, this is a Chinese restaurant. We serve Chinese food only."

"God damn, I miss Texas. Ella Sue, I reckon tellin' ya these Asian folks ain't got no beef steak. Them yellas eat bugs and bird's nest soup and whatnot crap."

"Big Bob, it's our honeymoon and I got a hanker'n for Chinaman food. Now sit your ass down," commanded Ella Sue, taking a firm grip on her new husband's arm.

Big Bob moved his lips as he read the menu. "I ain't partial to rabbit food. A real man eats meat 'n' potatoes," he said, tossing the menu on the floor.

Ella Sue shook her head with embarrassment. "Big Bob, in case ya ain't noticed, I don't have nothin' danglin' between my legs. I like Chinaman food and ya can't get decent Chinaman food in the hill country."

Big Bob gazed down at the chopsticks on the table, nodding his head in compliance. "Damn Chinamen must think we white folks don't clean our teeth often to put such big toothpicks on the table for us. I'll grab me a steak 'n' fries when I git back to the hotel, but I'll try some of that Chinaman rice wine I hear carries a good wallop."

They both removed their hats. Ella Sue looked over the menu.

"Hey, boy, where's the wall hooks for hangin' hats?" queried Big Bob.

Willie cleared his throat. "Sir, this is California. Most Californians do not wear hats big enough to hide an illegal immigrant."

The couple chuckled.

"Chinaman, you're as funny as cow manure on a stick," joked Ella Sue. She placed their hats on a nearby empty dining table.

"Uh, my apologies, you cannot place your hats on a vacant table. Others may wish to sit there."

The six-foot-four cowboy stood up to tower over the shorter waiter. Taking a hundred-dollar bill from his wallet, Big Bob shoved it into Willie's breast pocket.

"Boy, y'all pretend we got a couple invisible friends eat'n at the table next to us," Big Bob said.

Shocked by the couple's odd solution as to where to rest their hats, Willie smiled thinly. "Yes, sir. This table will be reserved for your friends," he said, placing a reserved sign on the dining table.

"Gettin' that settled, what's ya'all's recommendation?" Big Bob queried.

"All these *gwai lah* morons understand is chop suey and egg rolls. Tell them anything," said another waiter in Chinese to Willie.

Willie ignored the waiter's advice.

"Why not be bold and try chicken feet, bird's nest soup, and perhaps some Peking duck?" Willie said. "The soup is a seaweed nest, and the bird spit gives it a great flavor."

Big Bob slapped the table, cackling outrageously. "No

wonder ya Chinamen are puny lookin'. Yer grub ain't even civilized."

"Shut yer mouth. This ain't no different than you eat'n cow brains and scrambled eggs for breakfast," Ella Sue said.

"Well, least they're 'merican cow brains, Mrs. Buckhorn," said Big Bob.

"Chinaman, bring 'em on," ordered Ella Sue, ignoring Big Bob's remark.

Willie carted out the food. The entire body of a crispy skinned duck was placed before Ella, with its head faced toward her. She stared at the bird's vacant, blackened eyes.

"Miss, enjoy," said Willie, detaching the head from the duck's body, then placing it on Ella's plate. "Honored guests are served the head, very crispy," he said, grinning.

Ella could not be sure if Willie's statement was sincere or if he was mocking this blond Texan.

With trepidation, Ella bit down on the duck's bill. A warm grin appeared on her face as it made a loud crunching sound. "Not bad. Like a duck-flavored potato chip. But I'm not used to having my supper stare back at me."

Ella began slurping the bird's nest soup, then sampled the chicken feet. "Boy howdy, Chinaman. Ya people can sure fix fine grub. This bird drop'n soup reminds me of salty grits. Husband, don't be a stick in the mud. Try somethin'," she said, sucking on the bird's foot.

With reluctance, Big Bob popped a chicken foot into his mouth. "Ahh!" he cried, grabbing his throat. His faced turned blue.

Ella Sue became hysterical. "Help! Help! My husband's choking on a chicken bone. Somebody please help!"

Reacting out of instinct, Willie jumped behind Big Bob, wrapping his arms firmly around the man's chest and pressing his fists against his breast bone vigorously. The chicken foot shot out of Big Bob's mouth like a bullet, striking Ella Sue on the forehead.

"Damn imbecile Chinaman," cursed Ella Sue, rubbing the

knot on her head.

Taking a moment, Big Bob caught his breath. He then stood up with a menacing glare toward Willie.

"Chink, how dare ya strike my wife," said Big Bob as he swung his ham-like fist at Willie's head.

Instinctively, Willie ducked. Missing his mark, Big Bob lost his balance and fell like an ox. His huge bulk leveled two dining tables and their cowboy hats.

"Aaah! My back, my back! It's broken!" cried Big Bob, writhing in agony.

Grabbing her flattened Stetson, Ella seemed more concerned for her cowboy hat than her husband. "Idiot Chinaman boob, soiling a cowboy Stetson is the same as spittin' on the flag ah Texas."

Deeply embarrassed, Willie bowed his head respectfully. "Sir, missy, I am deeply sorry. I was only trying to help extract the bone from Mr. Bob's throat. There will be no charge. Please allow me to order you a good meal to go," he said.

The couple ignored the waiter's apology and compensation offer. Ella Sue meticulously reshaped her Stetson while Bob moaned with a pained face.

In a few minutes an ambulance arrived, requested by Ella Sue. As paramedics carried Big Bob to the ambulance, he incessantly ranted curses and racist remarks at the waiter, as well as the restaurant proprietor, and said they would be hearing from his lawyer.

"Willie, see what you've done? Those *gwai lah* buckaroos will sue my ass for every penny I own. I'll end up back in China working the rice fields again," exclaimed Mr. Wang, the restaurant owner. "I should fire your incompetent ass."

Glaring, Willie was more angered by the mishap than ashamed. "I saved that racist cowpoke's life, and I get sued and fired for it?"

"Willie, it's a *gwai lah* world we live in. Go to the hospital now. Offer the couple free dinners for as long as they're in eye fowl," ordered Wang.

"And if they do not want the free dinners?" queried Willie.

Wang's face turned red in anger. "Then kiss those *gwai lah's* white asses. Anything to keep them from suing me."

Willie hated the idea of kowtowing to *gwai lahs*, who he had distrusted and disliked all his life, but he needed the work to pay for the college courses he was taking. "Yassir, boss man. I's a goin' as fast as I can shuffle my feet," Willie mocked in a stereotypical black man's voice, mumbled too low for his employer to hear him. *I wish I had spit in their bird's nest soup,* he thought.

The bus to the hospital seemed much slower than usual, though the city buses were never fast to begin with. An elderly Chinese man shouted in Willie's ear, complaining he was mugged by punk *gwai lah* teenagers. Willie sat, oblivious to the old man's rantings, in deep thought that his future career as a chemical engineer was in jeopardy.

This cowboy who thinks he is John Wayne and his bitchy wife might sue me along with Mr. Wang, just for the hell of it, thought Willie.

He reflected on the cute *gwai lah* blond he was in love with at age sixteen, how the girl reminded him so much of Ella Sue. The girl of his youth never said any derogatory remarks toward him; rather, she acted as if Willie was invisible, ignoring him in their classes together, or when they passed each other in the school hallways.

Willie's grandparents, who encountered far more racial problems than he when they were growing up, always spoke with bitterness and contempt toward the *gwai lahs*. Their constant bad mouthing of the *gwai lah*s, and Willie's own sense of never belonging and inferiority, forever warped his view on humanity, and made it difficult to form a relationship with a woman of any race.

He mumbled various forms of apology from the time he stepped off the bus until he reached Big Bob's hospital room. When he entered the room, he was nervous.

"Aaah! You again, Chinaman! Haven't you done enough to my husband?" screeched Ella Sue, sitting vigilant beside her husband's bed.

"Mrs., uh...uh...Buckdeer...Buckhorn..." Willie stammered. "I'm so sorry. I'm just a dumb Chinaman. My employer wishes to offer you and your husband a free dinner for every night you remain in Frisco."

"Damn nervy Chinaman." Ella removed the boot off her right foot, sticking it in Willie's face. "This here boot is gen-u-ine ostrich leather. It cost me six hundred big ones. Ya all think Big Bob and I want a free dinner? Big Bob and I are suing ya and your boss for all yer egg rolls."

Bowing his head in despondence, Willie exited the room, knowing there was nothing he could say to improve the situation.

Though not seriously injured, Big Bob was heavily sedated to allow him to sleep.

"What would I do without my Big Bob?" Ella Sue whispered after Willie's departure.

Big Bob began talking in his sleep. "Ruby! Ruby! I love ya more than anything in the world, my Sugar Butt."

"Shit, ya bastard. Who the hell is Ruby? Ya called me Sugar Butt on our wedding night. Cowboy, you'll be sorry ya ever fooled with this Texas cowgirl," Ella Sue shouted.

She ran out of the hospital. Standing on the street corner, she began to hyperventilate. She felt dizzy and dropped to her knees, inhaling the cold, damp San Francisco night air.

"Mrs. Buckhorn, are you sick?" Willie asked. He sat a short distance away on a bench awaiting the city bus.

Embarrassed, Ella Sue stood up and smoothed her ruffled hair. "Chink, mind yer own frickin' business," she snapped. She felt distraught as she remembered that she had left her prized Stetson in the hospital room. Her mind was a jumble of bruised emotions.

"Hey China—uh, Willie. Sorry. It ain't right of me bad mouthin' yer race. I ain't havin' a good night."

"That makes both of us," Willie said. He smiled.

"I feel kinda naked without my Stetson. I left her in Big Bob's hospital room," said Ella, returning the smile.

"Ms. Buckthorn, uh, Buckhorn, you're quite beautiful with or without the Annie Oakley hat."

Ella Sue giggled. "Lots of cowboys have called me a handsome filly, but I reckon no one ever called me beautiful, not even Big Bob." She paused. "Willie? I never did finish that bird's nest soup."

Willie cleared his throat. "Ms. Buckhorn, I have to ask you plainly: Are you and your husband planning on suing my employer and me?"

Ella Sue swiped a friendly slap on Willie's shoulder. "Damn ya, I'm invit'n ya to have dinner with me. My husband's family gots more money than George Bush Sr. and Jr. combined. We ain't in need of more money. Now, flag us down a taxi, my yella friend."

Ella Sue and Willie returned to the restaurant.

"Missy Buckhorn," said Mr. Wang, bowing repeatedly as they entered the restaurant. "A million apologies for my employee's clumsiness. Lobster and champagne, on the house," he commanded to a waiter with a snap of his fingers.

"Forget the snooty city food. Bring me bird's nest soup," snapped Ella Sue.

Willie donned his apron.

"What 'n the hell ya think yer doin'?" Ella Sue said.

"Mrs. Buckhorn, my shift is not over. I must return to work."

"The hell ya are. I invited ya for supper. Sit yer ass down. Tell yer boss to add what he's payin' ya to my bill."

Willie bowed as he took a seat across from Ella. He felt nervous, having had no social interaction with a woman in over a year. He was afraid to look at Ella directly, and was uncertain what to say.

"Hot damn, a little soup on a foggy Frisco night," said Ella Sue as a waiter placed the bird's nest soup before her.

With gusto, she slurped down the expensive dish. "Been eat'n rare steak most of my life, and plan on eatin' big Texas steaks until I die, but this here bird's nest soup is damn fine grub." She lifted the bowl to her mouth to finish it off.

Willie covered his mouth to hide his chuckling.

"What's so funny, yella man?" asked Ella Sue.

"Nothing. It's just us Chinamen like to make loud slurping noises to show our enjoyment of the meal. You'd make a good China woman."

Ella Sue smiled oddly. "Willie, we can go to my hotel suite and learn to be even more yella," she said, reaching for his hand across the table.

Willie nodded his head with acceptance. A look of guilt flashed across his face as he tried to ignore the thought of going to a hotel room with a married woman.

"Pilgrim, carry me across to the promised land," she mused, as they stood before the door to her thousand-dollar-a-night suite at the Mark Hopkins.

Straining mightily, Willie hoisted Ella Sue in his arms. On unsteady feet, his 155-pound frame carried the only slightly lighter Ella Sue into the suite. Once inside, he lost his balance. Both he and Ella Sue crashed into a heap on the plush white carpet. Shaken, but not injured, the pair laughed hysterically at the comical mishap.

"Pilgrim, betcha there ain't many chunky heifers in China like me."

Catching his breath, Willie said, "I was born in California. I grew up in the redneck USA, in the Sacramento Valley."

"If that ain't a kick. You're almost 'merican, like Big Bob and me," said Ella Sue.

With gritted teeth, Willie rose from the floor, pulling Ella Sue up with him.

"*Gwai lah* idiot, I'm a frick'n American citizen, not almost."

Ella Sue wrapped her arms around him. "Sorry, Mr. 'merican. I reckon you want that piece of the 'merican dream.

Well, here is a Texas-bred dream."

Willie pecked Ella Sue on the cheek. "All my life I've wanted a piece of *gwai lah* ass. In Big Bluff, all the hot *gwai lah* babes chased the football jocks. They were never interested in a Chinese boy. I always wanted to play with the cool white kids. Then I came to eye fowl, which is Chinese for 'big city.' All of a sudden, I was surrounded by yellow people. They maybe looked like me, but that was about all we had in common. Even my yellow sisters didn't want me. I'm a freaky ABC—'American-born Chinaman.' Or worse, a banana—white on the inside and yellow on the outside."

Ella Sue began to unbutton Willie's shirt.

"My yella friend, ya ain't sure what you are. Hell, I reckon we're all lookin' for somethin'." She directed Willie's hand to her left breast. "Them snooty white bitches in Big Bluff ain't got nothin' on me."

Willie could feel Ella Sue's hardened nipple under her blouse. For a long while he massaged her breast. He began to feel euphoric, as if high on an illicit drug. It was the first happiness he had felt in years.

In a sudden about-face, Willie pushed away from Ella Sue.

"Willie, what in the hell is wrong with ya? There ain't no man in Texas who would not kill to bed me, less'n they been dead for three days," Ella Sue said.

"Something's not right, Ella Sue. You're a goddamn newlywed. Why bed me unless something has happened between you and your mutant cowboy husband?"

"Chink, I'm offerin' you a piece of the 'merican dream. No one says no to Ella Sue Buckhorn!"

She threw an ashtray at Willie, which barely missed his head. Willie snatched a bottle of tequila from the wet bar to throw in retaliation.

"Not the tequila, fool Chinaman! That's two hundred dollars yer wastin'."

"Sorry," said Willie, placing the bottle down on the bar

counter. "Ella Sue, I'm not sleeping with you. The cost is too high."

"Banana," mocked Ella Sue.

Willie smiled. "F. Scott Fitzgerald once said that there are some disappointments you can never recover from, except by becoming someone else. Someone who doesn't quite care as much about things they once cared about. I don't like being a banana. Goodbye, Mrs. Ella Sue Buckhorn."

"That Fitzgerald fella, he some tenderfoot hippie?" queried Ella Sue as Willie exited the room.

Two days later, Big Bob felt well enough for the couple to return to Texas. Eventually, Ella Sue found out that Ruby was Big Bob's beloved childhood pony. He had nicknamed her "Sugar Butt" because of the pony's white rump. Their marriage ended in divorce after only one year.

Willie met and married a Chinese girl who had arrived recently from mainland China. Having nothing in common, their marriage lasted only six months.

Willie and Ella Sue began e-mailing each other. She vowed to Willie that she would someday return to eye fowl for more bird's nest soup.

— The End —

The Laughing Mourner

The parade of mourners wailed so loudly that even the deceased they honored could hear them. At the head of the procession, mounted on a long pole, was an enlarged photo of the deceased. His finely decorated coffin rested upon a flower-strewn wagon drawn by two white horses. The dead patriarch, Too-sin, had been ruthless in his affairs and had made few friends during his life in the Middle Kingdom. Nonetheless, it was no surprise that a long line of mourners dutifully followed the wagon.

Most of the mourners had never met Too-sin while he lived. In fact, aside from the family and the marching band, many of the mourners were paid to be there. Such pretentiousness was quite common in China, where ancient customs and traditions died hard. Only the rich could afford such excessive showiness. It demonstrated to the world how beloved and significant the departed family member was, in both life and death.

Although such an ostentatious display did not fool many, it was an impressive spectacle. A marching band played to a clamorous crescendo as the funeral procession filed down the roadway, then stopped at the home of the deceased to pick up a wreath of flowers that adorned the front door—symbolic of the deceased visiting his cherished residence one last time before his journey to his just rewards.

At this particular funeral, an elderly woman of seventy-two named Song-she demonstrated such near-hysterical grief that one would have thought she was a close relative of the dead patriarch. That was not the case. Song-she was a paid mourner and a veteran of over one hundred such funerals.

She had learned early on that the greater the display of sorrow, the more money she was paid. Song-she had the talent to cry on cue whenever the occasion called for it. The ability to show such expressive emotion kept the elderly woman in great demand. And on this day she was in particularly good form.

"Too-sin was such a beloved and caring man. We will miss him so much. Life is unbearable without this beautiful man," Song-she eulogized, sobbing to the curious crowd that lined both sides of the street.

The long funeral procession culminated with a grand dinner at the village's public meeting house. As was customary, strong rice wine flowed freely and the food was plentiful for all those in attendance. With a sudden metamorphosis, the tearful mourners turned into festive party revelers. And as no paid mourner cried more sorrowfully than Song-she, no one laughed more heartily than Song-she at the stale jokes and anecdotes about the deceased.

"Ah yes, I remember quite well when Too-sin fell out of the persimmon tree as a young boy, landing upon a rather unfortunate sow pig," she mused in mock memory.

As the raucous crowd became distracted by a troupe of traveling Chinese opera singers and dancers, Song-she helped herself to the lavish food. She took particular interest in the Peking duck and suckling pig, as meat was a luxury few poor people in China could afford. Careful not to be noticed, she squirreled away tasty bits of succulent meat into a deep pocket she had sewn into her jacket specifically for such occasions.

The joyous Chinese wake would last well into the following day. It was past noon when Song-she returned to the plain, one-room apartment she shared with her teenage granddaughter.

"JeeJee!" Song-she cried in an agitated voice.

The listless young woman lay on an unkempt bed, earphones on her head, listening to a Britney Spears CD. She stared complacently at her exhausted grandmother.

"My lazy granddaughter! The pile of soiled laundry is still sitting where I left it yesterday," Song-she quipped. "Did I not make it clear that you were to wash the clothes before my return?"

"Grandmother, I've told you many times—you are to call me Britney," mused JeeJee. "I will someday be a rich and famous singer like the *lo fon* girl Britney Spears. Besides, I have much homework to do. I was merely resting my brain before I do battle with geometry."

Song-she glared at the lackadaisical teenager with burning eyes. "JeeJee…uh, Britney…perhaps you might want a little practice in routine work, incase your maid should take ill and you are forced to do the housework yourself," she retorted. "I am sometimes glad your parents are not alive to see what a disrespectful and unworthy young woman you have become."

JeeJee rose off the bed. She gathered up the pile of dirty clothes and placed them in a wicker basket. Her face was flushed with anger and her lower lip pouted like a small child's. "Dear grandmother, my parents would be disappointed in us both. You did not shed any tears at your own daughter's funeral, nor at my father's funeral. Oh, I forgot, Grandmother. You only cry at funerals when you are paid." JeeJee walked out the door and headed to the communal laundry room downstairs.

Song-she's withered face showed little emotion at her granddaughter's biting remarks. JeeJee's words cut her as deeply as a sharp knife cutting into her flesh, but the young woman's sarcasm was not without a ring of truth. It was true. Song-she did not cry at her own daughter's funeral. She could not say for certain why, even though she could cry on demand at the funerals of perfect strangers. Deep within her she knew that she subconsciously resented her daughter and son-in-law for dying before their time. Aside from being burdened with an unruly, impertinent child, Song-she felt angry and bitter that there would be no one to care for her in her declining years.

For centuries China had encouraged large families. It was understood that having a large family ensured that the parents would be cared for and provided for in their old age by their children. But Song-she was blessed with only one grandchild. There would be no one there to lift her up should the old woman fall, or to feed her when the years grew too heavy for her. What else could she do but carry on the way things were? Aside from her peculiar profession, she had earned a few yuan sewing and cleaning homes for the well-to-do, but arthritis no longer allowed her to do even those menial tasks.

Song-she's worries consumed her, but for the moment she took pleasure in knowing that she and JeeJee would eat well that evening with the fine food she had surreptitiously taken from the funeral reception. Eagerly, she set the table and prepared tea and rice for the grand meal.

"Grandmother, you always forget the plum sauce. You know I like it with my duck," complained JeeJee when she saw the duck parts sitting on the dining room table.

"JeeJee, you know how difficult it is for me to carry the sauce without it spilling on my clothes," Song-she replied.

"Britney! Britney! How many times must I repeat it? I want to be called Britney!" JeeJee fumed.

"My granddaughter, why must you pretend to be a *lo fon* whore? You are a shameful banana—yellow on the outside, white on the inside. Are you ashamed to be Chinese?"

JeeJee shot a searing gaze at the old woman. As she groped for a fitting response, a soft knock echoed from the front door. It was not often that Song-she had visitors, and her granddaughter, ashamed of their humble abode, seldom invited her classmates to visit.

Apprehensively, Song-she opened the door a slight crack, fearful the caller might be the landlord demanding the frequently late rent. But instead of the grumbling old landlord, a well-dressed woman in her late twenties peered back at her.

"Mrs. Tang, I assume?" she inquired. "I have need of your services. I know you are normally contacted by way of the local employment office, but I wanted to see you in person. You will do just fine. I am Su-sin Liu. My grandmother has died. It was so horrible. She died in bed." The young woman barged her way into the small apartment.

Song-she and JeeJee stared at the woman curiously.

"What is so horrible about an old woman dying in her sleep?" JeeJee asked.

"I did not say she died in her sleep. Mama Hag died in the arms of our ancient gardener. How disgraceful for a woman of eighty to have sexual relations! She even drank liquor!" Su-sin exclaimed. "Her soul was poisoned by too much *gwai lah* TV. However, she was my grandmother and I still love her in spite of her shortcomings. She must have a proper send-off. I understand that you are the best mourner in the region."

"There is no one in all of China who can show more sorrow and respect toward the passing of a loved one," stated Song-she proudly.

"Good. It is settled," Su-sin said enthusiastically. "I will pay you 200 yuan, double your usual fee. For your doubled fee I will expect you to give a brief toast at the reception following the funeral walk. Arrive promptly at Fung's Funeral Parlor tomorrow at noon."

"I will require additional time to write a speech to show the appropriate sincerity for your most beloved grand-mother," Song-she said in a businesslike voice. "I will need 225 yuan."

Su-sin looked slightly annoyed, but nodded her head in agreement. The willowy young woman walked to the door with an air of superiority and waited impatiently for someone to open it for her.

"Miss Liu," JeeJee said to the stranger with a mischievous grin. "Is your hand broken, or perhaps you do not know how to operate a door knob?"

Song-she was embarrassed by her granddaughter's mocking words. She raced to the door and held it open for her disgruntled patron. "Please forgive my granddaughter's disrespectful words. She is not well. A brick fell upon her head as she walked by a construction site yesterday," she said, unable to think of anything else to excuse JeeJee's ill manners.

A subtle, bemused look came over the rich woman's face. "I think more like the entire building fell upon your bitch of a granddaughter," Su-sin laughed. "Is your naughty granddaughter a professional mourner, as well?"

"I do not cry rivers of tears for people I do not know," replied the outspoken JeeJee.

"I will also pay this young lady 200 yuan. Mrs. Tang, your acid-tongued granddaughter reminds me so much of my grandmother. Her presence would indicate my grandmother's spirit lives on in China's strong young women," Su-sin said.

"Screw you! I am not my grandmother. I will not pretend to mourn over someone I have never met," JeeJee retorted.

"Two hundred yuan is a handsome sum for someone who is only seventeen!" exclaimed Song-she. "Miss Liu, I promise you that both my granddaughter and I will be present at your grandmother's funeral tomorrow."

Miss Liu nodded her head once again, then departed with no further words.

"I won't do it! It is beneath me! I will someday be a famous celebrity. I will not do a beggar's job." JeeJee shouted in defiance.

A sharp pain overwhelmed Song-she's body and soul. Fighting back her tears, she realized they had both been a disappointment to each other. She wanted JeeJee to attend the funeral with her not only for the additional 200 yuan, but also so her granddaughter might gain some understanding of the sacrifices Song-she made to provide for her.

"Jee…uh, Britney, please do this for me this one time," Song-she pleaded. "If you are to be a famous singer like the *lo fon* woman, this Spears you speak of, you will need a little money to move to *eye foul*, the big city. Certainly you cannot expect to be famous in Qin-dee. You will have to move to Guangzhou or Hong Kong."

JeeJee pouted as a small child would when being forced to drink a bitter medicine. "Grandmother, only this one time. Someday I will be so rich that I will spend 200 yuan for the *gwai lah* Starbucks coffee I saw advertised in a *Gim Sam* magazine."

On the following day the weather turned cold and misty, making a usually sullen event even more so. A huge, solemn crowd of paid mourners gathered at the funeral parlor. The sea of people dressed in black resembled a flock of crows assembled to feast on a dead carcass.

"We must all show proper respect," Song-she told the other mourners in her most authoritative voice. "Do not dawdle or make idle chat to each other during the funeral walk."

"Who made you general?" spoke an old woman named Mua. "I know proper manners at a funeral as much, if not more than you, Song-she."

Song-she sneered at her on-again off-again friend of several years. "Mua, sweet friend. Anyone who wears more makeup than a circus clown has no right to question anyone's authority," she said with a perverse grin.

"Better to look like a clown than a prostitute," Mua responded, glancing at JeeJee's clothes. "Only a lady of the evening would wear such a short skirt on such a chilly day."

At first JeeJee ignored the old woman's caustic remarks; then she slowly turned toward Mua and began chewing on a wad of bubblegum she had kept resting beneath her tongue. "Old bitch, my skirt is barely a foot above my ankles. You behave as though I were naked. Would you have me wear a heavy veil as the Muslim women do?" JeeJee blew a bubble and popped it loudly.

"Perhaps a veil would not be such a bad idea," replied Mua. "At least it would cover that hideous nose ring of yours."

"Ancient bitch! Your mother has bound feet. How is my nose adornment anymore ridiculous than having grotesque, rotting feet?" JeeJee shot back.

Reacting before tempers could flare even more, Song-she quickly placed herself between the two bickering women. "Stop this nonsense, both of you! We are here to honor a kind and beloved woman who passes on to her just rewards. Show some respect and dignity." Song-she turned to JeeJee. "Granddaughter, we will walk together arm-in- arm once the procession begins."

Mua rolled her eyes in disgust at her old friend's bossy nature, but chose not to make further waves. She stomped away to the back of the crowd.

The somberly dressed mourners formed a line on either side of the funeral parlor's walkway as the casket was carried to a beautifully decorated, horse-drawn wagon. The mourners bowed their heads in reverence as the pallbearers slowly passed.

The funeral of the matriarch Hag Liu was the grandest one ever held in the village of Qin-dee. The weeping members of the matriarch's family walked at the head of the procession, followed by the paid mourners. Young dancers dressed in white flowing togas pranced about, throwing sweet-smelling rose petals into the air. Two men set off firecrackers at the end of each block, and a marching band vociferously played China's national anthem. The impressive fanfare was meant to announce to the heavens that the old woman would soon arrive.

"Mama Hag was the best friend ever! She was an angel in human form!" a weeping Song-she shouted to the hundreds of spectators lining the streets to watch the spectacle. Beside Song-she was JeeJee, stepping lively to keep pace with her grandmother. The teenager spoke no words of praise for the woman she was paid to mourn. In fact, she looked quite bored and detached by the entire event.

Song-she pinched her granddaughter's left arm.

"Ouch!" screamed JeeJee.

"My actress granddaughter, act like you've just lost your best friend. You have no more emotion than if we were bidding farewell to a cockroach!" whispered Song-she through clenched teeth. "Cry, dear granddaughter!"

JeeJee responded with an agitated frown, but complied with the old woman's command. Burying her face in her hands, the stubborn girl wailed loudly, giving the impression she was sobbing, though no tears flowed from her eyes. "Oh, poor Mother Hag! We all loved you so much. Why did you have to leave us so soon?" she cried. For added drama, she extended her hand to touch the casket. In doing so, the gangly young woman lost her balance and crashed to the ground. Her fall brought the procession to a complete stop.

No one was more dismayed by this accident than Song-she. Only moments before her granddaughter's spill, Song-she felt for the first time a genuine sense of pride and fondness for JeeJee. Though her arthritic hands and arms ached terribly, Song-she swiftly lifted her embarrassed granddaughter off the ground. The old woman's concern was not for her own personal discomfort, or even for JeeJee's well-being; her only thought was how her exacting employer was going to react to this awkward mishap.

"Take your hands off me, Grandmother! I am not a baby! Goddamned platform shoes," JeeJee muttered. "My best black dress is ruined. I should make the Liu family pay for it."

"Incompetent idiot!" shouted Su-sin, approaching to see what had halted the funeral walk.

"I am so sorry, Miss Liu," Song-she said. "My grand-daughter did not mean to disrupt your grandmother's funeral. It was an accident. JeeJee is of a simple mind. Please forgive us, honorable lady." Song-she clasped her hands together, begging for forgiveness.

"Grandmother! You play me as a village fool so that you can save your job?" exclaimed JeeJee. "I do not grovel for anyone, especially this snobbish bitch."

Feeling deeply insulted, Song-she slapped her insolent granddaughter. "JeeJee, I have tolerated your disrespect long enough. Miss Liu's grandmother has died. Please show proper dignity and courtesy to Miss Liu and her family." She paused, then added, "Your parents were inconsiderate to die young and leave me to care for a selfish brat!"

JeeJee stared at Song-she with a look of shock and pain. She fought the urge to cry, but relented to a single tear that ran down her cheek. "Grandmother, I will no longer be the heavy stone upon your shoulders," she said. "Miss Liu, may I have my 200 yuan?" she asked in a matter-of-fact voice.

Miss Liu counted out the appropriate sum and tossed the wad of money at the teenager. "Go!" she said.

As an afterthought, JeeJee removed her platform shoes and handed them to Miss Liu. "Here. You need to accessorize better, Miss Liu," she quipped in a mocking tone. "Rest in peace, Mother Hag," she said. She kissed the coffin, then stormed off barefoot. "Goodbye, Grandmother," she called over her shoulder without turning her head to look back at Song-she.

The street was silent. Everyone looked at one another in bewilderment.

"Mrs. Tang, you are also free to leave. Here is 300 yuan," said Miss Liu, placing a thick stack of paper money in Song-she's hand.

With her head hung, Song-she walked away in humiliation. She did not dare speak to or look upon her fellow mourners. In turn, the other mourners did not dare glance a sympathetic eye upon the embarrassed old woman, for fear that doing so would jeopardize their own livelihoods, as well.

Song-she returned to her cold, dark apartment. As expected, JeeJee was not there. It had been a difficult and strange day. Song-she's joints ached more than ever before, and she could not bear to turn on the light knowing the room was void of any life other than her own.

From that day forward, Song-she was no longer in popular demand as a professional mourner. She still received occasional funeral work, but at a greatly reduced fee. Though she had never been in good accord with her absent granddaughter, she now missed her sharp-tongued irreverence. She yearned for a human voice. Her small circle of friends had abandoned her, labeling the old woman bad luck. Song-she was lonely.

Soon a year had passed since her granddaughter had left her. Often she would ponder whether JeeJee had gone to Guangzhou or Hong Kong to become the model or actress she had dreamed of. A warm smile would cross the old woman's face as she envisioned her granddaughter being rich and famous. But reasons for Song-she to feel joy were few and far between. With each passing day she became weaker and more pained from her arthritis and her increasing problem with heart disease. Most days she would lie on her bed, unable or unwilling to leave it.

On one such day, a day that began like all the others, Song-she heard the deafening sound of a brass marching band and firecrackers. A grand funeral! From her bed, Song-she wondered how they could give the deceased a proper send-off without her.

"Who in Qin-dee is so important to have such a boisterous funeral procession?" she said aloud.

The professional mourner's curiosity got the better of her. Unable to walk, she slid off the bed and crawled to her small balcony. Her gnarled hands painfully clutched the top of the rusted railing. Fighting for her breath, she pulled herself up to catch a glimpse of the procession.

By now the open casket was passing directly under her balcony. Song-she squinted her weak eyes to see who had died. She could make out an old woman dressed in fine, embroidered silk clothing. The face appeared serene and unburdened by life's struggles. Then, something else caught

Song-she's attention.

"It is me!" she exclaimed, catching her breath. "Oh, it's me!"

With disbelief, the old woman struggled to get a better look. She saw her old friends and fellow funeral mourners parading after the coffin. She saw JeeJee walking beside the funeral wagon. The young woman raised her head and gazed at the balcony. Grinning widely, JeeJee blew her grandmother a kiss.

Song-she chuckled and returned the smile. A sense of peace filled her tired body. Then, with the glorious sound of the funeral procession filling her ears, her eyes closed and her frail body fell lifelessly onto the balcony floor.

— The End —

Round Eyes

"Who is that *gai jin*? Her eyes are like fried eggs!" Ecko Aoki asked her girlfriend, Rue Okawa. The two young women stared intently at a thirty-foot digital image of a fiery, redheaded Caucasian woman gleefully inhaling an American cigarette on a giant screen over a boulevard in Tokyo.

"She is the famous *gai jin* movie star Bette Davis," explained Rue. "She's dead, I think, but she's still popular in *gai jin* land. She's peddling a new round-eye cigarette called Waiting to Exhale."

The short, stocky Ecko began to giggle. "This is the *gai jin's* idea of beauty? She looks like a clown in drag. She makes a *Harajuku* girl look like a nun."

The even plumper Rue rolled her eyes in frustration. "Girlfriend, that *gai jin* earns millions of yen with her big eyes while we are struggling to survive on the tips we earn at the coffee shop."

Ecko chuckled. "Good friend, we must be immense failures indeed if a dead *gai jin* earns more money than us," she mused. "We Japanese are lost. We've grown tired of our jet-black hair and narrow eyes. But suppose we all looked like white-rice girls with blond hair and blue eyes? Would we not also eventually tire of the sameness? Who made the *gai jins* rulers of the universe?"

Rue glared at her friend contemptuously. "Girlfriend-San, you simply do not understand. I do not want to look *gai jin*. I just want round eyes. I am proud to be Japanese, I just don't want to look like one."

"Ha! You make no sense, my friend. Why not expose

your ample breasts in public if you wish to be noticed?" Ecko declared.

Ecko's close friend smiled coldly. "My robust friend, you mock me. You challenge me with such a silly dare for you think I would not do such a thing," quipped Rue. "Notice this, girlfriend!" Rue ripped open the front of her silk blouse, exposing her pendulous breasts. "Look at me, my Japanese brothers and sisters!" commanded the twenty-nine-year-old coffee server to passersby.

To Ecko's dismay, her fellow countrymen and women, being of a reserved nature and overly polite, ignored her friend's risqué and irreverent exhibition. She swiftly buttoned her friend's blouse. "Rue-San, dear friend, you silly girl. This is Japan. People wouldn't notice you if you were a hundred-foot-tall Godzilla."

Rue sniffled, then dropped to her knees, sobbing uncontrollably. "Girlfriend, we are destined to die alone, yes?" she asked her friend in a wavering voice.

Ecko kissed her friend on the lips. "Rue-San, the world does not revolve around the two of us."

"With our expansive waistlines, I would think a moon would orbit around us," Rue chuckled as she stood.

"Nice tits," exclaimed a passing eleven-year-old *gai jin* girl, licking an ice cream cone.

Ecko and Rue both rolled their eyes, then resumed their stroll back to their jobs as baristas at one of the 100-plus Starlite coffee shops in Tokyo.

"You're late from your lunch break," said the girls' boss, Heedo. "I will dock you both one-half hour's wages."

"Our deepest apologies, Heedo-San," said the girls in unison, bowing their heads in atonement.

The tall, balding man viewed his subordinates contemptuously. "Honorable bitches, you should be sorry. I've promoted Akee to morning shift supervisor."

Rue and Ecko stared at him with disbelief.

"But Heedo-San, you promised one of us would be given

the morning supervisor position!" exclaimed Ecko.

"I've had second thoughts. You two squid-brains are simply not management material. Your eyes appear unspirited and untrustworthy. Enough said. Now, get to work while you still have employment at Starlite."

The two friends were in a state of shock.

"Akee is only twenty and has worked at Starlite only six months. She is so unworthy to be promoted over us. I can prepare a green tea frap that people would commit *sepku* for," Rue proclaimed bitterly.

A shrill, sinister laugh could be heard behind the girls' backs. Turning swiftly, they faced their new supervisor, Akee. The much taller, thinner, and prettier young woman towered over her slighted underlings.

"Congratulations, Akee," stated Rue.

"Congratulations, Akee," stated Ecko.

Both girls wore forced smiles.

"Is there something different about you, Akee?" Ecko queried, examining the young woman with close scrutiny.

The new supervisor, who had adorned her face with heavy makeup, grinned smugly. "Ah, Miss Aoki, you noticed my beautiful new eyes. They are rounded like Manga cartoon characters. I will give those *gai jins* Mariah Carey and Britney Spears some competition," she giggled.

"But honorable Akee, you were very beautiful before you had your eyes corrected."

The new morning supervisor, standing tall with forty-inch legs, brushed aside the coiffed hair that covered her left eye. "Dwarf!" she exclaimed. "Do not question my decisions regarding my personal growth—or anything else of significance or insignificance. Get to work, now, before I have the two of you walking the streets wearing heavy sandwich board advertisements."

As ordered, the girls diligently went about their duties, busing dirty cups and sweeping the heavily soiled floor, which needed constant attention as a result of the polluted Tokyo air. Out of the corner of their eyes they observed their new boss applying lipstick and meticulously arranging her silky hair as she gazed vainly into a compact mirror.

"When Akee was getting her eyes fixed she should have instructed the doctor to implant a new personality into her, as well," mused Ecko under her breath.

Rue stuffed a napkin into her mouth to muffle her laughter.

Like most days, the coffee shop was bombarded with a steady stream of coffee enthusiasts, mostly young college students attending nearby Tokyo University. Ecko and Rue began to notice that many of the well-dressed students' eyes appeared more rounded than the usual, narrow Japanese eyes.

"Hey, you hormone-imbalanced Sumo wrestler! One grande Chantico with extra whipped cream, a teaspoon of soy, a light sprinkle of cinnamon and chocolate shavings. And I only want seventy percent cocoa chocolate," commanded a male preppie whose neck was wrapped with a finely woven alpaca scarf, most likely worn for adornment rather than comfort considering the sultry weather.

Ecko stood rigid for a moment, offended by the young man's hurtful remarks. She carried on a silent conversation with herself as to whether to retaliate with an equally caustic reply, or to simply ignore the man's rudeness.

"Ah, yes sir, right away, sir," she said, stepping quickly and choosing submissive politeness rather than putting her job in jeopardy. As she handed over the Chantico, Ecko sensed something familiar about the obnoxious customer. "Sir, have you been to Starlite before? I think I have seen you, but I cannot place where and when we've met."

The pretentiously dressed young man eyed the barista with a self-satisfied grin. "I was once a mouse who dreamed of being a man. And now I am one. My eyes are circular and quite handsome. I'm a hot guy," he proclaimed, raising his eyebrows to make his eyes appear even rounder.

A surprised look crossed Ecko's face. "Huh! Now I

remember. You were the studious boy whose face was forever buried in engineering books. You wore glasses, and like a timid puppy, you were afraid to look me in the eye when you ordered."

"Most certainly; but now I am god-like. I had surgery on my eyes to make me a beautiful man. I hope to marry well and earn a billion yen before I am thirty. I'm so hot I'm on fire," he mused. "Ahhhh!" he suddenly screamed as an elderly woman poured iced coffee over his head.

"Young man, I could not bear to witness a fellow Japanese on fire. I felt compelled to cool you off," quipped the old woman, holding back her laughter.

Ecko herself fought the urge to laugh at the impertinent man's comeuppance. Greatly embarrassed, the young student stomped out of the coffee shop at a loss for words. The elderly woman gave Ecko a sympathetic wink.

"My respectful thanks to you, dear madam," said Ecko.

"Young woman, someday the world will love narrow eyes and robust bodies," the old woman predicted kindly.

The barista appreciated the old woman's soothing words, but knew such a future promise seemed unlikely. Throughout the day Ecko served numerous other patrons whose eyes had been altered and whose demeanor seemed to have changed as a result. They had become more extroverted and confident— some to the point of arrogance, as in the case of the insolent young student who had come in earlier.

"The people with new eyes seem much happier. No doubt happier than I am," Ecko mumbled under her breath.

When the difficult workday finally ended, Ecko and Rue rode together on a musty-smelling, cramped city bus to their homes in a poor section of Tokyo. Their houses, which sat side by side, resembled mere cubicles made of plywood and tar paper rather than genuine houses.

"Ecko! Just in time for dinner," stated Chako, hugging her eldest daughter. "Father has returned with a special treat for us! Double Big Macs with fried potato sticks."

"You mean French fries. That is what the *gai jins* call them," corrected Ecko with a polite though insincere smile. She gazed down at the bags of fast food that sat on the dining table held up by cinder blocks.

"Yes, yes, I keep forgetting the *gai jin* words for those fried things," cackled Mother.

"If this Western delicacy is French, why is it not bathed in heavy sauce?" queried Mito, the fifteen-year-old younger sister who closely resembled a younger version of Ecko.

"Little sister, forget such nonsense. Perhaps the Americans do not want to take complete credit for making the world fat," Ecko commented.

"Let's eat," said Mother, ignoring the girls' bantering.

With gluttonous abandon the Aoki family sat upon fluffy pillows and gorged themselves on the high-calorie food. With disposable bamboo chopsticks the family smothered the fried potatoes with catsup, then dipped them in soy sauce before eating them. They spoke infrequently, thus allowing themselves more time to dine on the food they cherished so much. Their bloated faces resembled the face of the blowfish, a Japanese delicacy.

"Mamma-San, pass me the wasabi, please," Ecko said, her eyes finally meeting her mother's.

There was something strange about her mother's face. Gradually Ecko's eyes shifted to her father's face, then to her younger sister's. Perplexed, Ecko's mind raced as she examined with close scrutiny the faces of the people she had lived with her entire life.

"Mamma-San! Papa-San! Little sister! What has become of your eyes!" she exclaimed.

"Ah, my eye is slipping!" cried Mito, rushing to the bathroom with her mother in tow.

"Not enough glue," said Papa-San oddly between mouthfuls of fast food.

"Not enough glue," mimicked Mama Chako, quickly returning with Mito.

"I am now a hot infant again, as the *gai jin* say," proclaimed Mito.

"You mean a 'hot babe,'" corrected her father.

"What is this nonsense you speak of?" Ecko asked.

The barista's family chuckled outrageously.

"Silly daughter, this mysterious glue we speak of is to lift up our extra eyelid fold."

"It's the latest craze for those who cannot afford an operation to have their eyes permanently rounded," explained Mito with giddy enthusiasm.

Ecko shook her head with disapproval. "If *gai jins* had a third eye, I believe we Japanese would have eyes implanted into our foreheads," she chided.

"Don't be absurd, daughter. Who would we get to donate the eyes to us?" commented her father.

"Enough foolishness!" said Ecko's mother. "For dessert we have apple pie!"

"Ah! Ooh!" exclaimed Ecko's ecstatic father and younger sister.

Exasperated, Ecko leaped to her feet. "My loving family, you do not even like apple pie!" she remarked, storming out of their hovel.

The young woman wandered about the immense city. For the first time she noticed how many things her fellow Japanese had adopted from the Western world, from eye alterations to blue jeans and blond wigs. Though no words were exchanged, Ecko sensed an air of superiority from the faces of those she passed. In heated anger and disgust she climbed atop a bronze statue of Mickey Mouse adorned as a Samurai.

"Brothers! Sisters! Have you all lost your senses? Have you all gone mad? Why must you forsake your identities, your heritage, in order to feel good about yourselves?" she exclaimed, straddling Mickey's head, her plump arms gripping the mouse's ears tightly.

"Come down, lady," shouted the one sole spectator. "I'm

not sure who appears more buffoonish—you or the mouse you are sitting on."

Glancing down, Ecko was taken aback to see that she had only gained the attention of a single *gai jin* man. As before, when Rue had bared her breasts, the Japanese continued about their business. In a small country crammed with 185 million souls, they had learned long ago to build invisible walls around themselves in a place where solitude and privacy were rare commodities.

"Who are you?" she asked.

"An ugly American named John Smith," the man said with a silly laugh.

Ecko gazed curiously at the lanky, clean-cut young man. "I've never heard of such a *gai jin* name. Is it common?" she inquired.

"As common as apple pie," John chuckled.

"Do not speak of such Western excrement! Help me down," she commanded, reaching out for the man's hand.

The stranger reached his right hand upward to grip Ecko's hand. In flip-flops, her feet slipped and she lost her balance as she bent to grasp his hand.

"Ahhh!"

With a crash she fell on top of the surprised man.

"Clumsy *gai jin* fool!" Ecko cried.

"I beg your pardon, my Japanese friend. You fell on me, not the opposite," John informed her as he helped Ecko to her feet. "My apologies. We Americans do not always succeed in saving the world," he finished wryly.

Ecko smiled nervously, feeling guilty over her rudeness toward a perfect stranger. "Smith-San, I am sorry. You tried to help me and I acted badly," she said, red-faced and looking down. "I've lost face."

John Smith glared at the Japanese girl with cold disdain. The stranger pulled a thousand-yen bill from his pocket and placed it in Ecko's hand. "Young woman, buy yourself a new face."

"Smith-San, I am an impolite mother of a dog," responded Ecko.

"No apologies necessary," cackled John. "We Americans have been rude to other races of the world for centuries. By the way, I think the term you were referring to is 'bitch.'"

"'Bitch' is not a nice word, yes?" queried Ecko.

"Yes, not nice unless you really are a female dog with puppies," mused John.

Ecko smiled with a girlish giggle. "Smith-San, we must start fresh," she said, thinking how odd it was that so many *gai jins* had such pasty skin and thin lips. "Why do you come to Nippon?"

"Nip...? Oh yes, Japan! I am the proprietor of a chain of fast-food eateries from the U.S. Fried Bob's Goodies. Our specialty is deep-fried Twinkies. If my research is correct, your people will die for this wonderful tidbit," Smith stated with great enthusiasm.

Ecko flashed him a disapproving smirk. "No doubt my fellow citizens will die for such a delicacy, as so many of my friends and family have already died from your Kentucky Fried Chicken and Big Macs," she said candidly.

"Who wants to live forever?" stated Smith with a philosophical grin.

Ecko laughed loudly. "I do not want to live at all. Perhaps dying by fried Twinkies will grant me a more honorable death than the death of my grandmother, who stabbed herself in the throat. Ritual Japanese suicide. Men being men must kill themselves the messier way, by slitting open their stomachs."

"Miss, I think I like the 'death by Twinkie' option more than the stomach trick," John responded.

Ecko smiled politely and turned to walk away.

"Hey miss, before you die by your own preference, would you share a Chantico with me? You are most hot. Please?"

For a moment Ecko stood assessing the young American's invitation. "What do you mean?"

"Ha! Chantico is a very rich chocolate," John said,

grinning widely.

"I know what Chantico is. I am an honored barista at the Starlite coffee shop. What do you mean, I'm 'hot?' Am I on fire?"

The young man began chuckling. "Miss, it is American slang meaning attractive. You're also cool."

"Cool?"

"Disregard my foolish American pleasantries and simply understand that I would like to know you better. Now, what about that Chantico?"

"I do not make friends with round-eyes," Ecko stated with a harsh glare.

The young man responded with more a look of fascination than offense. "You're racist," he said, amused.

"Sir, I am only a fat, ugly Japanese woman. Why would I feel superior to anyone?" Ecko walked away feeling disturbed over her soul-baring confrontation with the Caucasian stranger.

After traveling two blocks, Ecko was startled to notice John Smith walking only a few feet behind her. She wasn't sure what to make of the annoying stranger. It had been a great while since any man had asked to join her in anything. In fact, she had never had a real boyfriend—ever. She turned to face John. "Chantico. One Chantico? You ask nothing more of me?" she said in a halting voice.

"Nothing else. I am alone in cherry blossom land and I know no one here," John replied.

The pair blended into the hoards of humanity that crowded every primary street in Tokyo. Ecko did not completely trust John Smith, but simply allowed him to take her hand as he led her to the nearest coffee shop. It was a Starlite. The employees there knew her as she had worked there on occasion filling in for someone ill or on vacation.

"Sit down, Smith-San. I will prepare the Chantico myself," Ecko said, heading for the counter.

"Ecko, I didn't think you had a fondness for *gai jin* men," commented a barista who had known her for years.

"It is not your concern," she replied. "I am not a banana; white on the inside and yellow on the outside. Do not speak ill of me. You are the one who has changed your eyes, not I." She directed her scolding words toward the acquaintance who had often mocked her for her short stature and plumpness for as long as they had known each other. The woman turned her back and pretended not to hear Ecko's criticisms.

Ecko placed the cup of thick hot chocolate on the table before Smith, and another Chantico across from him for herself.

"Why do you want to drink Chantico with me? I'm not pretty. I look like a woman Sumo wrestler," Ecko asked shyly.

"Miss Madam Butterfly, I have not yet had the pleasure of knowing your name." He placed his right hand gently over hers. "Why shouldn't I have an interest in you? I love fat— uh, big-boned women. A woman need not look like a supermodel to be interesting."

The timid young woman was flattered by the man's attention.

"Smith-San, I am Ecko. I think you are interesting, too," she giggled.

"Pleased to meet you, my new friend Ecko. I've heard Japanese girls giggle a lot when they're in the presence of a man they're attracted to," he said, smiling warmly.

Giggling even louder, Ecko covered her mouth and blushed.

"Close your eyes," John said. "I have a gift for you."

Ecko did as instructed. She felt the man flatten out her hand with the palm facing up. Then she felt something light in her hand, with a rough texture. Puzzled, she closed her fingers around the unknown object. It felt spongy, yet had an odd slickness. Totally confounded, Ecko opened her eyes to find what looked like a deep-fried piece of dough. Grease oozed from the object and dripped small puddles onto the table.

"What's this?" Ecko asked with a frown.

"Ha! It's the greatest food innovation since the caveman decided cooked meat tasted better than raw. It's a Bob's deep-fried Twinkie. Please, take a bite."

Cautiously, Ecko placed the sweet morsel into her mouth and gingerly bit off a small portion. The soft marshmallow-like filling blended provocatively with the crispy outside cake layer. A pleasant smile crossed her lips. Voraciously she consumed the remainder of the treat. "Smith-San, your fried Twinkie has a good taste. However, it is much too obvious that such a heavy fried food is not good for the body. But one on rare occasion should not be disastrous."

"Excellent! I will have my PR man contact you. He will get a mug-shot of you along with your complimentary quote," exclaimed Smith.

Ecko glared at Smith with contempt and hurt. "Smith-San, you are nice to me only so I can praise your Twinkie product?"

"I…I…of course not," stammered Smith.

Two baristas recognized Smith from the business page of a Japanese newspaper. "Hey, cute guy! You hire us, please? We have pretty big eyes like real Manga cartoon characters."

Ecko fumed over her colleagues' rude intrusion. The *gai jin* man smiled widely.

"Ladies, Fried Bob's Goodies always has room for such beautiful women. My middle name is Bob. Please call me Bobby," John said with a flirtatious wink.

"Smith-San, you didn't finish your Chantico," Ecko said. "If it is too much, take what remains with you. It is on me. Or, it would be more correct to say it is on you, Smith-San." And with that, Ecko calmly poured the beverage in the man's lap.

"Holy shit!" cried Smith, leaping to his feet in agony. "You crazy bitch!"

"You call me a mother dog again?"

Swiftly, the two other baristas appeared with towels and a

pitcher of cold water.

"You poor man," said one girl as she and her associate vigorously rubbed the dark, soggy stain on Smith's pants.

"Ecko," said the other girl. "You are an evil woman. Because of you, this man won't have a family!"

"Adopt, you loose-face! Buy a new face, Smith-San!" Ecko said, tossing a wadded 100-yen note onto the table. Stomping out of the coffee shop, Ecko crossed the street and entered a bar. She ordered a bottle of sake and began to gulp the strong liquor directly from the bottle. "My people are lost. They should be more like me, Ecko Aoki," she muttered under her breath.

"A thousand pardons, miss," said a well-dressed Japanese man, placing his business card on the table. "Allow me to introduce myself. I am Isao Isigho, talent scout for Japan's *ichiban* reality show, *Loser's Challenge.* We pit less-than-perfect ladies against each other for a date with the man of their dreams. The winner also receives a free surgical eye enhancement. You would make a perfect contestant."

Ecko grimaced while staring at the sake bottle, not wanting to look at the man.

"Young lady, you would be the envy of even Bette Davis if you win the free eye operation. If she were alive, that is," Isigho chuckled.

Ecko continued to ignore the persistent man. Growing impatient for some response, Isigho placed a 1,000-yen bill before her.

"Miss, I know time is money for all of us. Please accept this money to hear me out. The *Loser's Challenge* is most popular. All contestants on the show become instant celebrities, and if you should have the good fortune of winning the elimi-date show, your eye correction will make you a new woman. I might even persuade my superiors to include a week at Japan's top health spa. Not to say you're unattractive, but you could stand a little adjustment."

An offended look immediately flashed across Ecko's face.

"But I am unattractive, and you and your bitch boss are simply having people like me make fools out of ourselves for profit."

"Dear woman, nothing can be further from the truth. We want to honor imperfect people by making them perfect. We do not mock them. Incidentally, I believe the *gai jin* term 'bitch' only refers to females. My boss is male," Isigho said with a silly grin. "I do not mean any disrespect, but I suspect you have already been mocked and laughed at in your life. I will sweeten your bowl with a million yen. This will just be between you and me."

The insecure woman sensed the man's false sincerity. She despised the way so many of her fellow Japanese had adopted and even obsessed over the *gai jin* culture and their appearance, as if to imply that their own race and nationality were inferior to the Western culture. But the lure of easy money and the prospect of being the center of attention for the first time in her life was tempting.

Before she could respond, Isigho placed his business card into the palm of her hand. "Come to the studio tomorrow at noon. Soon you will be fighting the groupies off with a bamboo rod," he predicted.

Ecko was stunned and speechless as the talent scout hugged her, then kissed her firmly on the lips before departing. She sat on a barstool staring at the gold-embossed card. Fighting her demons, the young woman crumpled the card and tossed it onto the floor. She walked with determination toward the exit, then stopped suddenly, blocking a small group of patrons waiting to enter the sushi bar. The barista made an about-face and stepped slowly back to her table. She retrieved the wadded business card and slipped it into her left bra cup.

"Today a coffee waitress, tomorrow a round-eyed sex symbol," she mused.

That night Ecko said nothing to her family about her future fame. They paid little attention anyway, what with their attention directed toward a Sumo tournament on television. The next morning Ecko sat with her family for their normal breakfast of green tea and Krispy Kreme donuts.

"I'm quitting Toyota," her father announced. "I have grown tired of picking up other people's trash. I want to work for the *gai jin* Wal-Mart. Then I will be a man of great honor."

Ecko's mother and kid sister, both wearing blond wigs as they often did, stared at him with shock and disbelief.

"Papa-San, if you were to work for Wal-Mart I believe you would still be picking up the trash of others," remarked Ecko.

"But it would be *gai jin* trash!" her father exclaimed.

"Soon *gai jins* will be picking up my trash," Ecko remarked.

The family stared with confusion at Ecko's puzzling remark.

Later that morning she boarded a city bus for her trip to the TV station. During the long ride she sat with a troubled look on her face, uncertain of whether she had made the right decision. She was perspiring and her heart pounded rapidly as the bus gradually came to a halt a few blocks from the TV station.

As Ecko approached the station she was taken aback to see two women at the entrance even more obese than her. *They resemble bloated porcupine fish. If that is my competition, I will shine like the best Mikimoto pearl,* she thought.

A man dressed as a Samurai poked his head out from behind the door. "Welcome, honorable contestants, please come in!" he said with a wide grin. "Allow me, respected ladies, to introduce myself. I am Hootie Karoake, the host of *Loser's Challenge.* Your destiny awaits you."

The women were quickly escorted to individual dressing rooms. A matronly, conservatively-dressed woman began stripping Ecko of her street clothes. As they stood before a full-length mirror, the woman placed a vivid pink wig on

Ecko's head, complimented by an equally gaudy costume of bright colors. Then two younger women rushed in and whisked the anxious Ecko to an adjoining room. They threw her into a padded swivel chair. In a frenzy, one of the women began applying heavy makeup to Ecko's face.

"Miss Aoki, aren't you so wonderfully beautiful," exclaimed the makeup artist. She spun the chair to face the mirror.

Ecko's mouth dropped with shock and humiliation when she saw her reflection. "You have transformed me into a *Harajuku* clown!" she exclaimed, wiping the caked makeup onto her sleeve.

"Madam, do you realize how expensive that dress is? The cleaning bill will be outrageous!" shouted the makeup girl.

"I am not a dancing bear! I will not be your fool for the sake of TV ratings!" Ecko replied.

"What is the meaning of this?" Hootie asked, entering the makeup room.

"This horrible woman thinks to be dressed as a *Harajuku* is demeaning. As if being fat, short, and unattractive is something to be proud of," whispered the makeup girl.

"I heard that!" exclaimed Ecko.

Embarrassed that the contestant had overheard her mocking remarks, the makeup girl made a hasty exit.

"Miss Aoki, pay no attention to that woman. She is Korean. Koreans are uncouth, barbaric people. We Japanese are going through a cute phase in our history. Being *Harajuku* is merely one form of the Japanese ideal of being *sugoi*," voiced Hootie.

"Ha! We're lost, not *sugoi*. We do not know who we are. You cannot force me to be a cartoon!" Ecko stated, thrusting the pink wig at Hootie.

The TV host rolled his eyes with exasperation. "Very well, Miss Ecko-San. I will not force you to be cute. I can only hope our fans will approve of such blandness." He turned to his assistant. "Give the street clothes back to Miss

Aoki and the other contestants," he ordered.

"I will be treated with respect, yes?" Ecko asked, removing her costume.

The TV host exited the room without a reply.

Ecko and the other contestants rode in a stretch limousine to an upscale Tokyo nightclub. Hootie stood beside the entrance along with hundreds of rabid fans. The girls were blinded by countless camera lights as they exited the limo.

"Ladies, it is time for your fifteen minutes of fame," mused Hootie, giving each contestant a bear-like hug.

A TV cameraman followed the girls and Hootie into the club. A tall, athletic man dressed in an all-white Armani suit sat with his feet on the table, sipping a glass of Sapporo beer. He winked at the contestants as they entered.

"Ladies, I give you Elvis Taro, Japan's greatest racecar driver. Please sit and relax a moment. Two of the other contestants have yet to arrive," said Hootie.

"Such a pleasure," said Elvis, kissing each woman's hand. "Where else but Japan would women with such little sex appeal have an opportunity to date a man of my stature and good looks?"

Ecko wasn't surprised to see that the celebrity had had his eyes widened like so many other Japanese.

"Save a kiss for us!" called a familiar voice.

Ecko spun around and was dumbfounded to see her friend Rue standing before her.

"Rue! What is your business here?"

"Ha! Ecko, what is *your* business here? Did you not inform me recently in so many words that Japanese are lost Asians searching for an identity? Japanese need to look like Japanese, is this not so?" Rue said, demanding an answer.

Ecko could scarcely look her close friend in the eyes. "Rue, my good friend, I apologize to you and all of my Japanese brothers and sisters. To change the shape of one's eyes is no different than applying mascara. I have lost face,"

Ecko said, bowing her head humbly.

Ecko's friend began to chuckle in amusement at the unexpected change in values. "Friend, are you speaking from the heart or has the heavy sack of yen the show is paying you swayed your reasoning?"

Insulted, Ecko shoved her friend. Rue fell backwards and was caught by a TV assistant. With equal anger Rue pulled her right arm back to swing at her friend, but a thunderous applause from the fans outside the nightclub distracted her.

Making an entrance befitting a rock star, another familiar face entered the nightclub. It was Akee.

"Rue and Ecko, I did not expect to be competing against a couple of dwarfs!"

"Akee! You can't be serious about wanting to be a contestant on this show! You're too beautiful to be here!" said Ecko. "Besides, you're our boss at Starlite. It would not be proper."

"Ah, how delightful! The three of you know each other!" Hootie said, laughing over the absurd coincidence. "This will make the competition even more entertaining. I will dismiss the other contestants. Just the three of you shall compete."

Akee glared smugly at the two stout women with an arrogant confidence that said she would most certainly triumph over them. "My plump friends, I was a former contestant on *Loser's Challenge*. Like the two of you, I was an unnoticeable, insignificant blob. After winning the contest I was transformed into the goddess I am today. I won the eye operation and liposuction, and I am now competing once again to win a boob job. My breasts will be as lovely as the perfect *gai jin* Pamela Anderson," exclaimed Akee, laughing menacingly at Rue and Ecko.

Both girls gazed down at the floor with demoralized dejection.

"Let the show begin!" proclaimed Hootie.

The three women sat at a low round table with the racecar driver. An array of sushi delicacies and warm sake adorned the table.

"Feel free to acquaint yourselves, ladies, with Japan's most spectacular racecar driver," Hootie said.

Taking the initiative, Akee straddled Elvis's lap, filling her mouth with sake and swishing it around in her mouth while giving Elvis an amorous wink. The aggressive woman wrapped her arms around him, then pressed her lips firmly against his, transferring the sake from her mouth to his. Startled by her boldness and choking on the strong wine, Elvis coughed harshly, spraying the faces of Rue and Ecko. Elvis looked at the girls, dismayed.

"Ignore them," Akee said, licking the man's wet face. "They're only flunkies in my coffee shop."

Feeling more offense than flattery from Akee's flirtatiousness, Elvis jumped to his feet, knocking Akee off balance and causing her to bump her head on the table. "A thousand pardons," he said, taking a cloth napkin and wiping the sake off Rue's and Ecko's faces.

"Elvis, it is of no consequence," Rue said, blowing him a kiss. "I would prefer to be spit on by the most handsome man in all Japan than be given a string of Mikimoto pearls."

Uncomfortable in the circus-like atmosphere, Ecko brushed aside the napkin that patted her face.

"Elvis-San, how can you favor these two carp-faced women over me?" asked Akee, rubbing her aching head as she rose from the table.

"Excuse me, honorable boss," Rue said. "You appear to have lost a portion of your breast." She pointed to a falsie that had popped out of Akee's blouse and was now floating in a finger bowl.

With excited embarrassment Akee swiftly snatched the falsie and stuffed it back into her bra. "Ah, it's…uh, a protective device for my breasts," she stammered with a nervous grin.

"Protecting them against what?" inquired a bemused Elvis.

"To protect her from loneliness, I suspect," commented Ecko. She stood and turned toward the exit.

"Please, Miss Aoki, do not leave," Elvis said. "You are most certainly a woman of substance and I wish to know you better."

Ignoring the man's pleading, Ecko walked onto the busy, smog-choked boulevard. Trailing her closely was Elvis, along with a TV cameraman, Akee, Rue, and the groupies and fans of the reality show.

"Please, Miss Aoki, stop! I choose you. I want no other. Please," Elvis begged, scurrying to catch up. "Please stop. Let's discuss this."

"Elvis, you will not deny me my large American breasts!" screeched Akee, leaping onto the man's back.

"Crazy woman! Get off my back!" Elvis exclaimed.

"Elvis, please accept me," pleaded Rue, blocking his way as he struggled down the street after Ecko with Akee glued to his back. "I will be even more beautiful than Akee when I have the eye transformation."

Clumsily, the trio fell onto the sidewalk. Turning to look back at the commotion, Ecko cackled at the entangled heap of humanity.

"Get that ridiculous camera out of my face!" screeched Akee as she awkwardly rose to her feet. "It was ordained by the producers that I would be the winner!"

Elvis assisted Rue up from the ground, then grabbed Akee suspiciously, whispering in her ear, "Akee, my love, the producers felt it best that one of the fat, ugly girls should win this time. Better ratings. Sorry, Akee."

A sleek black Lexus limousine pulled up to the curb. Hootie jumped out of the car. "Excellent! Our viewers will eat this up like free sushi! Are we having a good time, contestants?" he asked with a smirk.

"Bastard! I deserve to win!" Akee screamed repeatedly, attacking the show's host with her purse. "I have lost my beautiful breasts!"

"Lady, lady, my pretty cherry blossom," Hootie said, wrapping his arms around her as if to comfort her. "You will have your breast augmentation. The show will pay for it. Plus you will receive two-million yen for your trouble."

Akee broke free from his grip. "Very well, have a good life, pretty boy! Sayonara!" she said.

As soon as Akee left, Rue rushed forward. "Elvis, my passion. My girlfriend Ecko is too set in her ways. She will break in a strong wind, unlike myself, who bends. With new eyes I can be the woman you desire. Choose me, Elvis-San. I beg you."

As with Akee, Elvis strongly embraced Rue. "Rue, the producers have already decided Ecko will be a better match for me, but like Akee, you will have the operation you desire so much and will be compensated with half-a-million yen. One hundred thousand more than Akee," he said softly into Rue's ear.

A subtle smile formed on Rue's face. "How delightful that I will be paid more than my snooty, self-loving boss."

Believing the lie, the appeased woman bade her friend and Elvis goodbye and departed in a taxi.

Rabid fans of the show and the famous car racer began to swarm around Ecko and Elvis, pleading for autographs from both. Refusing to be distracted by his fans, Elvis gripped Ecko's hand and pulled her into Hootie's limousine. Frightened by the frantic attention, Ecko crouched down in the backseat of the car. She began to sob uncontrollably. Elvis placed his hand on her back and began to massage her with care.

"Woman, pull yourself together," he said. "This is show business. I will make you as famous as Godzilla."

"Miss Aoki," Hootie said. "You must take notice of Elvis's words. If you wish to sit at the table of the beautiful people, you will do as we ask." He blew a couple of rings of smoke with each drag he took from his long, gold-stemmed cigarette holder.

"Will I be loved?" Ecko asked shyly.

Both Hootie and Elvis began to chuckle.

"Silly plump girl," Hootie said. "This is show business! It is not love. It is fame and billions of yen!"

"My new girlfriend, you will be surprised at how many friends fame and a mountain of yen can buy," added Elvis.

A confused Ecko peered out of the tinted car window. A mass of onlookers surrounded the car, hoping to get a peek at the well-known celebrity and his newest conquest. "Hootie-San, I will do whatever you ask of me," sighed Ecko, watching the spectators become increasingly smaller as the limousine sped away.

Giving no notice or reason, the handsome racecar driver planted a wet, sensuous kiss on the lips of the shocked young woman. Ecko's mind was a jumble of mixed emotions; elated that an attractive celebrity would display strong affection toward her, but at the same time angered over his brashness.

As Hootie predicted, the reserved barista soon became a popular celebrity. She and Elvis became an intriguing item whose every move was observed and recorded by Japanese paparazzi and the tabloids they worked for. Ecko's televised cosmetic operations were the highest rated TV programs that calendar year. With liposuction, the widening of her eyes, and custom-made, bright aqua contacts, Ecko Aoki had gone through a complete metamorphosis. Her family and what few friends she had had only tolerated her constant whining and melancholy before her transformation, but now they were fawning sycophants over the new Ecko.

As her fame ascended, so did her finances, with countless business entities requesting Ecko's endorsements for their products or services. Even the Playboy subsidiary in Japan contacted her for a nude layout. She began to laugh and cry simultaneously in reflection of the deep depression and loneliness she had known her entire life, and how now, as one of Japan's most famous and beloved women, she was insanely and deliriously happy. The one exception was during her infrequent private moments when feelings of self-doubt and lack of self-worth would consume her soul.

I am so happy...I think I am happy... thought Ecko as she raced by a massive billboard depicting her grinning image endorsing a dried squid product. *I am loved by so many...I think...* she thought, returning waves to admirers who recognized her as she continued to cruise along a wide Tokyo boulevard to cut the ribbon at the opening ceremony of a shopping mall. Her relationship with Elvis was beginning to cool, although with delusional expectations she had joyfully informed reporters of her impending marriage to the racecar driver.

"We love you, Ecko-San!" came the collective cries of the shoppers at the mall opening.

"When will you and that gorgeous racer marry?" came a voice from the crowd.

"When I finally get a free moment," Ecko replied.

Besieged by autograph-seekers, Ecko began to notice fewer of her fellow Japanese with altered eyes, blue contact lenses, and bleached hair.

A young girl of six tugged on Ecko's white silk Versace. "Are you Japanese?" asked the diminutive girl.

Startled by the question, Ecko didn't respond. Snatching a newspaper from an outstretched hand, Ecko began to sign her name. Then she stopped, shocked, before she completed her name. She was holding a seedy tabloid in her hand. On the front page was a photo of Elvis Taro embracing a fair-skinned, *gai jin* woman. Staring at the photo, she began to feel both ill and perplexed. There was something odd about the *gai jin* woman's face. Why did her eyes appear so thin and her hair so abnormally black-black? Only her pointy nose and lean lips revealed that she was indeed Caucasian. Without returning the garish paper to the autograph-seeker, Ecko stormed away without explanation.

"Miss Aoki, you cannot leave!" exclaimed the mall director. "You are being paid a handsome yen to ceremoniously open our new mall. You haven't even cut the ribbon yet!"

Ecko stopped and turned to face her benefactor. "Honorable Director-San, it is most urgent that I leave. My house is on fire," she said with a serious face, then turned her back to him and marched to her car.

Ecko knew Elvis was shooting a TV commercial for the newest craze, glow-in-the-dark cigarettes, in the ancient city of Kyoto. It was near nightfall when she reached the set. Crew members milled about making preparations for a night shoot. The man she had once loved so dearly was seated in a director's chair with the beautiful, exotic-looking *gai jin* woman sitting on his lap. The affectionate couple seemed out of place with a revered Shinto temple in the background and Japanese sika deer feeding complacently on green grass a short distance away. The woman took a drag from the novel cigarette. The couple giggled as she blew the smoke into Elvis's mouth, oblivious to the clamorous sounds of the set workers' tasks and the wrathful Ecko approaching them.

"Elvis-San, are you and your egg talking politics?" said a tearful Ecko.

A startled Elvis began choking on the strong smoke.

"Smoking is not good for your health, my love," mused Ecko.

"Bitch!" screeched the *gai jin* woman. "How dare you call me an egg! I don't know what it means, but I am certain it is something rude."

"White on the outside, yellow on the inside, but I think some of your yolk is bleeding out," retorted Ecko, tossing the sordid newspaper at the woman.

"Cut! Cut!" shouted the director. "How impertinent of you to interrupt my creation!"

"Toshee, you egocentric prima donna. The cameras are not even rolling yet!" shouted Elvis, pushing aside his new lady friend. "Brittney, my *ichiban*, please rest a moment in the dressing trailer. Miss Aoki and I need to sever the cord that binds us together."

The *gai jin* woman planted a loving kiss on the man's lips, then brushed past Ecko, blowing her a contemptuous kiss. Elvis took Ecko by the hand and led her for a stroll along a placid pool filled with brightly colored koi fish.

Visibly upset, Ecko fought to regain her composure. "Elvis-San, we were lovers. Why do you betray me in this manner?" she asked, brushing away her heavy flow of tears.

Elvis held Ecko tightly, her sobbing face pressed against his chest. "Miss Aoki, you are a lost Japanese woman. You need to reclaim your heritage in order to have genuine serenity," he said in a calm, soothing voice.

Angrily, Ecko released her arms from the only boyfriend she had ever known. She stood rigidly and glared at him. "My former lover, where did you get this piece of Zen philosophy, a Manga cartoon?"

Elvis began laughing with great amusement over their absurd lives and circumstance. "My Japanese sister, I have found enlightenment and I pray you will find it as well. Ecko, my yellow sister, the narrow look is the latest statement in *gai jin* cool. The greatest *gai jin* goddess Madonna is having it done. And I myself will have my eyes made to appear thin, it is so erotic-looking!"

Ecko was dumbfounded by his irrational remark. "Elvis, darling, your eyes were that way originally."

"Of course, most certainly. We do whatever is necessary to remain hot. That means…"

"I know what 'hot' means," retorted Ecko.

Elvis took a firm hold of Ecko's right hand. "Ecko darling, in order to remain famous there are things I must do. I mean no offense when I say that you are not hot. But to show no bitterness between us, give me one last kiss, my dear Ecko-San." Elvis puckered his lips.

"Yes, one final kiss for my first and only love. Close your eyes, Elvis-San," Ecko said, smiling softly.

As requested the man closed his eyes and a smirk-like grin

crossed his face.

Without hesitation the embittered woman gave Elvis a forceful shove instead of a goodbye kiss. Elvis cried out with surprise as he crashed backwards and splashed into the koi pond.

"Elvis-San, you are now cool as well as hot," Ecko chided.

The following day Ecko scheduled cosmetic surgery on her eyes, this time to have her original, heavy-lidded eyelids restored. "After my operation I will be truly hot!" she said as she arranged the date of her operation.

— The End —

The Three Gorges

"I do not want to go to the Gobi. They cook with camel shit and drink spoiled horse milk. Besides, the land is boringly flat!" exclaimed the weathered and shabbily dressed fisherman, Gim Shay.

"Old friend," Fat Lee proclaimed, "we were both born and have lived all our lives in the Three Gorges, and we both made a good life fishing our beloved Yangtze. But the world spins with or without us, dear friend. The 600-hundred-foot dam is nearly completed—a great lake will soon fill the gorges. There is nothing that the two of us, or even God, can do about it. I suppose it is for the best. The Yangtze has killed thousands of our fellow countrymen over the centuries—plus the great dam will light a billion light bulbs in China."

"Fuck the dam," cursed Gim as the two fisherman drifted lazily downriver to a small village harbor. "Our lives are what we make of them—no one forced us or the millions of others to live on land that constantly floods. Oh yes...fuck the light bulbs, too. I have lived my entire life without light bulbs and I have fared well."

"Gim, our time has passed," Fat Lee quipped. "Soon we will no longer be able to fish or feel the sheltering stone walls of the canyon. It is our sacrifice to China and the world. It is progress. We are both sixty years of age and the fishing has not been productive for the last five or six years. The increased boat traffic—so many tourists as well as the dam workers and materials being shuttled to the dam site—has corrupted the waters and frightened the fish. Do we have any other choice but to be relocated to the Gobi?"

Gim responded with a scornful gaze. "To hell with you, Fat Lee. You use the *gwai lah* tourists and whatnot as an excuse because you have lost your touch. You have grown old. Your mind is like the thin rice soup my wife cooks too often."

A hearty laugh bellowed from Gim's old friend. His tall, lanky body doubled over as his chuckling echoed along the canyon walls. "I'm old? Gim, you fool! You are the same age as I. If I am old, then you are also old."

"When we reach solid ground we will see which one of us is old," smirked Gim.

"Gim, my sweet friend, you are a silly old man. You are still angry that I used to bully you when we were children. You could never best me in anything. Did I not catch the largest fish on this and several other days? When the government relocates us to the Gobi, I will raise better sheep than you, or grow better rice than you, or whatever the shit our benevolent government will choose for us to do there."

Gim's ancient fishing boat pulled into the little harbor. For a few minutes he was speechless as he reflected upon his friend's biting words. What Fat Lee had said had a taste of truth to it. But then Gim Shay had never gotten the better of anyone in his life. "Go to hell," he blurted, unable to think of anything clever to say.

"You've already asked me to go there," smiled Fat Lee. "We will both visit that place together when we settle in the Gobi."

As the tiny boat coasted to the dock, the two fishermen stared dumbfounded at a well-dressed, attractive young woman. She was accompanied by a man holding an enormous television camera. They were surrounded by curious local villagers—most who had never seen a television camera before.

The woman extended her hand to Gim Shay. "Mr. Gim Shay, how delightful to meet you. Permit me to introduce myself: I am Suzie Kwai. I am a reporter for the National

News Service of China."

Gim ignored the young woman and hastily secured the boat to the dock. Embarrassed by the unwanted attention, the old fisherman and his comrade gathered their catch. They said nothing and avoided the gaze of the female reporter as they began to walk up the plank to the shore.

"Uh…please, Mr. Shay. If you will stand still for a moment I can inform you of wonderful news that will change your bleak and destitute life forever," the woman said breathlessly as she and the cameraman rushed to keep up with the two men.

Fully annoyed at the pestering woman, Gim abruptly turned to face her. "Damn it, young lady!" he shouted, his face only a few inches from her microphone. "What does a beautiful young city woman want with a bleak and destitute old man who smells of fish guts? Leave me alone. Go to hell."

The young woman stared with shock at the crusty fisherman's indignant demeanor. "Sir, you have been chosen to be the Three Gorges poster man. You will be on national television and in all of the major magazines. Mr. Shay, you will be a celebrity like Jackie Chan and the famous *gwai lah* Donald Duck. And of course, you will be paid handsomely for your endorsement of the government's relocation program." Miss Kwai spoke in a very persuasive manner.

The woman towered over Gim's five-foot, 150 lb. frame. He stared blankly at the reporter for a moment, then at the television camera. "I have fish to clean, and my wife will show great anger should I be late for dinner," he said, brushing the camera aside.

"But, sir! You are the chosen one. Your rugged, earthy face was pictured in the great *gwai lah* magazine *National Geographic*. The world already knows you. It is your civic duty to ease the minds of your 15 million fellow countrymen and women who will soon be displaced by the most monumental construction project since the Great Wall." Miss Kwai finished in a scolding tone, "Your people and your country need you."

Gim continued to walk briskly away with his stringer of fish slung over his shoulder. "Miss, you do not listen well. I told you to go to hell, and my 15 million countrymen can go with you. I am a fisherman. I do not serve horse manure for people to eat on television." Gim turned his back and walked up the plank to shore.

The exasperated young reporter could only shake her head with frustration as she watched the stubborn, unpleasant man walk away.

"Miss, please excuse my friend," said Fat Lee. He placed his hand on the shoulder of Miss Kwai's expensive dress suit.

"Sir, that is a 500-hundred-dollar *lo fon* Armani jacket your disgusting hand is touching," bristled the woman as she pulled his hand away. She smelled the fabric to see if it smelled like fish.

"Pardon me, lovely lady. As I was saying, my good friend Gim Shay is a simple-minded man. In fact, he stuttered as a child. He does not possess the ability to be a spokesperson for pickled chicken feet." Fat Lee paused for a breath, then continued, "I am a handsome, virile man and I would be a most worthy representative of our great country," he proclaimed, again resting his soiled hand on Miss Kwai's shoulder.

The young woman glared at Fat Lee, her eyes burning with annoyance. "Sir, you have a bloated ego and you smell of fermented fish paste. I would not have you as our spokesperson even if you were willing to dance with a circus bear naked at Tiananmen Square," she quipped.

Fat Lee's jaw dropped with astonishment at the young lady's candor.

A voice came from the crowd, "Miss! Miss! Please—I can be your spokesperson. I speak good. I am pretty. I will make the whole world love the Three Gorges Dam," shouted a plain-looking, heavy-set woman of twenty.

"I will be your spokesperson for half what you would pay Gim Shay," cried another voice from the packed throng.

The newswoman and cameraman rushed to a waiting van, followed closely by the zealous mob.

"Take me! Take me!"

"I will be your spokesperson!"

A cloud of dust obscured the crowd of eager villagers as the van raced away.

As the vehicle climbed the precipitous canyon road, Miss Kwai, overwhelmed by the maddening experience, looked at the small village of Qin Din and the caramel-colored river beside it. Its features grew less distinct as they drove away.

"It seems so ludicrous that the only citizen of Qin Din who does not wish to be the government poster person for the relocation plan is the one that the government's hierarchy has chosen," she said. The young and ambitious woman knew her promising career would be in jeopardy if she could not convince the curmudgeon Gim Shay to be the government's spokesperson. "The government wants an unpretentious, earthy, honest man, but they have picked something closer to a village idiot!"

It was near sunset when Gim finally arrived at his one-room house, which really amounted to nothing more than a pile of rocks assembled into a cube. The brittle wooden door creaked annoyingly as he swung it open. His wife Sin was sitting at a small table, gulping with gusto a bottle of Double Happiness beer.

"Another meager catch—it is scarcely enough to buy a handful of wormy rice. But it's no longer a worry, anyway," Sin smirked as she continued inhaling the costly beer.

Gim stood glaring with disgust and confusion at his wife's remarks. Gim's wife had been a beautiful woman when they married as teenagers. Like most attractive young girls, Sin's family had expected her to marry well—but misfortune unexpectedly reared its grotesque head on the eve of her sixteenth birthday. She was raped by a handsome suitor she had one day hoped to marry. The tragedy forever tainted Sin's chances of ever marrying into a well-to-do family and providing honor and wealth for her family.

Forever shunned by the eligible young men of Qin Din and disowned by her own family, she married the slow-witted Gim Shay out of spite—as well as desperation. Gim Shay himself was often the brunt of the villagers' ridicule and mockery.

Sin did not love Gim, nor did he love her. Though he was of a simple mind, the harassed fisherman knew a beautiful woman such as Sin surely married him for reasons other than love. But it was of no difference to Gim—after all, what other woman would want a stuttering fool? And after a few fleeting years, few men would want Sin. The once-beautiful woman had been replaced by an embittered, obese woman plagued with a nervous twitch in her right eye. Though it was a loveless marriage, they had remained together for four decades. Like so many other couples, they found their relationship preferable to loneliness.

Gim Shay was fuming. "You purchase Double Happiness beer? You know we cannot afford such luxuries! And what do you mean it is no longer a worry?" He threw his stringer of fish into a sink.

Finding humor in her husband's question, Sin burst out laughing, showering him with the costly drink. "Do not toy with me, my soon-to-be famous husband. A smartly dressed young woman named Suzie Kwai came here this morning looking for you. She explained that you were picked out of thousands—perhaps millions—to be the Three Gorges Project poster celebrity." She began to laugh hysterically. "I knew that silly photo of you in the *gwai lah National Geographic* would bring us luck someday. We will soon have enough Double Happiness beer to swim in." Sin fought to contain her chuckling. "We have both been looked down upon by the high-minded asses of Qin Din long enough. Now it is our turn to look down upon them. If our great country still had an empress, she would kiss your ass!"

A subtle grin crossed the fisherman's face. "If China still had an empress, she might wish to kiss *your* ass—there would be so much more area for her to place a kiss," chortled Gim.

Sin's wide grin transformed into a sneering contempt. Her right eye twitched as it often did when she became angry.

"I am sorry, my lovely wife, to make a joke of your generous size. It was cruel and I am sorry," Gim said. "But no one will want to kiss our asses, or any other part of our bodies. I told the young woman you speak of no. Perhaps it is fitting that the drink you have is bitter in taste."

The old fisherman's wife trembled from the revelation. The bottle of beer slipped from her hand and crashed to the floor, bathing her bare feet with beer and broken glass. Although her feet began to bleed from the shattered bottle, her anger was so vivid that she did not even feel or notice her wounds.

"My beautiful, wonderful, providing husband, I have lived in this shit hole for forty years and you have demanded I season all our food with gallons of soy sauce. How all that salt did not kill us a good time ago, I do not know. And now you say you have pissed away our one chance to live a double-happiness life? You are a stupid, fish-breathed idiot." She lifted a chair and threw it at her husband.

Gim ducked as the chair flew within inches of his head. For what seemed an endless, silent eternity, the long-estranged couple stood eyeing each other with glaring hate and disgust. At long last Gim broke the silence.

"My loving wife, I would not have done what you have asked of me. I was laughed at by the villagers for too long. I do not wish to be laughed upon by the whole world."

Sin giggled in a silly manner. "Fool husband, you would have been paid a hundred thousand yuan. We could have moved from this pile of rocks you call home. I want to wear pretty clothes and own a cell phone like the people in Shanghai. Why must you ruin everything?" she screamed, wiping away large tears, her right eye still twitching nervously.

"What is a cell phone?" Gim asked.

Sin rolled her eyes in frustration and resentment. Too angry, and dizzy from the excessive beer consumption, she spoke no further words to her husband. She displayed no emotion as she stepped on the broken glass and flopped dejectedly onto their bug-infested, unkempt bed. Her eyes closed tightly and she fell into a deep sleep.

Gim was used to his wife's rantings and biting complaints, but her eruption on this night seemed more unreasonable than ever before. Trying to block the difficult day from his mind, Gim went about his nightly routine of gutting and salting down his freshly caught fish. Once these chores were completed, the tired and confused fisherman sat down to a simple meal of goat cheese, bok choi, and white rice. Sin had left one bottle of Double Happiness untouched, and he heartily drank it with his meal. The cool beverage was his only respite from his hard day.

His muscles and bones seemed to ache more severely in the cold, damp weather than they did in earlier years. Gingerly, Gim lay on a mattress that sat in one small corner of the room. Rarely did he share a bed with Sin. Even more rarely did he make love with his wife.

Though tired, he had difficulty sleeping. In the faint flickering light radiating from the open stove, he watched his slothful wife for a while as she snored loudly.

Gim reflected on his life—whether it had been wasted, and if his wife, who he felt nothing for, had wasted her life, as well. Maybe he should have accepted the offer to be a spokesperson. A hundred thousand yuan was a lot of money. But even at age sixty, the memories of his childhood ridicule were forever etched into his mind and soul. He could not bear to ever be stared at or laughed at again.

Though Gim's stuttering had faded in early adulthood, he had yet to defeat his demons. Like so many that were riddled with insecurities, he had constructed an invisible wall around himself. To become a public figure meant crumbling that wall.

For even a strong, secure man it would be difficult to be unafraid of the additional burden—that his way of life and his very being would soon be erased. His life as he knew it and his home would soon be under hundreds of feet of frigid lake water.

Gim knew no other skill than fishing. What would he do? Would the Gobi be the nightmare that he envisioned? *Grow radishes*...Gim thought with a muffled laugh as he remembered Fat Lee's joke about what the two men would do in the Gobi.

Gim's eyes began to moisten as he resisted the urge to cry. He lay motionless in the dark. Throughout the night he looked up at the ceiling, his face distorted in a frozen grimace. He had slept only briefly when the alarm clock rang.

Sluggishly, his head drooping, he walked outside into the offensive cold air of early morning. Cradling a small bundle of split wood, he returned to his stone house to build a fire in the stove. Once the pile of short, dry wood and tinder began to burn in earnest, Gim placed a blackened kettle of water and tea leaves onto the grill. As he waited for the strong tea to boil, he munched on cold salted fish and a slice of hard, darkened bread. It was a simple breakfast that Gim had not varied in years.

The old fisherman chewed his breakfast and drank the stout tea with large slurps as he watched the low-lit fire, almost mesmerized by it as it crackled and popped.

Sin remained sleeping as Gim slipped out quietly to begin another workday. Slung over his right shoulder was fresh-cut bamboo that he had used for fishing rods since he was a young boy. In his left hand he carried a lantern to light his way, although he had walked the same path in the predawn, indigo darkness so many countless times he could have made the journey to his boat blindfolded.

"Gim, you are on time as usual," Fat Lee said, arriving at the boat dock shortly after his friend. "You're so predictable.

Does it seem colder than in past years, or am I just getting old? If you had good sense you would no longer need to feel the cold or rise before the sun ever again, my friend. Were you not the stubborn carp brain that you have been since we were children, you would now be living the good life with double happiness."

Gim showed little emotion toward his partner's criticisms as he readied his boat for the day's fishing trip.

"You're an idiot, Gim Shay!" exclaimed Fat Lee, angered by his friend's lack of response.

"Everything I need is here," Gim replied. "We are here to fish. Leave me alone!"

Gim shoved the boat away from the decayed wooden dock, no longer able to control his anger.

"But old friend, everything here will soon be gone. I would have given anything to no longer worry if I will catch enough fish each day to feed my wife and children," Fat Lee said as he maneuvered the boat in the current. "But you are right, my fishing companion—we are here to fish, not to bicker with each other."

Once in the main channel, the two fishermen drifted quietly down the languid stretch of the river. The sun greeted the two shivering fishermen as it made its debut over the south rim of the canyon.

The duo knew every deep hole, boulder, and eddy of the river. Anchoring at a favored hole, the two men set out a dozen bamboo poles. Their bait was rancid fish entrails mashed together with raw dough into a very potent-smelling round ball. Skillfully, they flung their heavy-weighted lines into the deep, swirling pool. From experience they allowed just enough line so that each ball of bait would rest upon the bottom without excessive slack.

Though the years of knowledge and practice had made the two men successful fishermen, the river traffic had become much heavier in recent years. Additionally, the mounting pollution entering the river had made catching fish far more difficult.

Hours passed lazily without so much as a nibble. Gim and Fat Lee's voices soon became hoarse from cursing at the passing ships and motorboats as their heaving wakes soaked them and threatened to swamp their tiny vessel.

The sun was soon high overhead, burning the fishermen's skin even more offensively than the sharp cold they had felt only hours earlier. It was at the hottest hour of the day that, at long last, Gim noticed the subtle tick of a fish bite. Reacting instinctively, he quickly grabbed the bamboo pole as it bent toward the water in a deep arc.

Pulling the pole hard over his right shoulder, Gim felt the weight of a heavy fish. "Shit! It's a fish of great size, this I am sure of!" screamed Gim as he held the taut line.

"Don't let him get away," commanded Fat Lee. "It may be the only fish of the day. Keep his head up!"

Gim cast an indignant look toward his long-time companion for giving advice to a seasoned fisherman who clearly had the ability to battle a large fish.

The angry fish began a long and determined run. The line ran through Gim's hands with such speed that his palms began to bleed as he squeezed it tightly to slow the fish down. Bracing his feet against the side of the boat, Gim pulled with all the strength his aching body could muster. Slowly, in small increments, the fish begrudgingly began to yield.

After an hour of battling, the spent fish raised to the surface on its side, its gills heaving desperately as it fought for breath.

"Great fuck, it's a silver carp! At least seventy pounds! I have never seen such a carp of that size!" Fat Lee exclaimed.

Gim's eyes brightened and his mouth formed into a wide grin. It was the first moment of real joy he had known in a long, long while.

"He is defeated!" Fat Lee said. "You have him! You will not be laughed at now. I think that even I would never again chide you or laugh at you!"

The wonderful trophy was nearly in Gim's grasp. The excited fisherman entertained thoughts of how envious the villagers would be when he paraded the enormous carp through the streets of Qin Din. Carefully Gim pulled the exhausted fish toward the boat. When the carp was within an arm's length, Gim reached down to gain a firm hold on it. He shoved his left hand into the fish's gaping gills and struggled to lift the heavy fish into the boat. Fat Lee leaned over the edge of the boat to assist his friend.

Suddenly, without due warning, a loud blast from a boat horn pierced the serenity of the gorge. The unexpected and unwelcome commotion gave the immense fish reason to rally. It dove to the bottom in a quick burst, snapping the line that connected fisherman and fish. Gim fell over backwards and bumped his head on the edge of the boat.

Dizzy from the fall, the old fisherman heard the youthful voice of someone he had hoped never to hear from again: "What a big fish! Too bad he got away," said Suzie Kwai, standing on the bow of a government-owned speedboat.

Gim splashed cold river water onto his face to regain his senses, then spun around to face the reporter. "Bitch! Damn cursed bitch. I have lost the greatest fish I have ever fought, and because of you, I have lost something that would have held great memories for the remainder of my life. I curse you. May all your children resemble that fat-lipped carp I just lost."

The young woman responded to the fisherman's angry words with a giggly bemusement. "My new friend, do not trouble yourself over one stinking fish. Soon you will be able to purchase a hundred carp the size of the one you have lost. Furthermore, it is unlikely I will bear carp-faced children. I do not plan to marry or have runny-nosed children. I am a career woman. Besides, we have much bigger fish to boil, Mr. Shay."

The more the young lady spoke of Gim's bright future the more infuriated he became with her enthusiastic demeanor.

"Miss Kwai, you are far too young to have a hearing problem. Did you not hear the word 'no' fall from my mouth yesterday? And why did you not go to hell? I think even the devil would find you too annoying to have around."

"Yes, I understand. 'No' has the same meaning in Hong Kong as it does in your backward village. But Mr. Shay, I have in my hand a government paper where 'no' actually means 'yes.'" Miss Kwai smiled as she waved the paper at Gim.

"The government cannot force the sky to be a different color," Gim replied.

The newswoman laughed at the colorful fisherman's naïve belief about the government's lack of power over him. "Foolish, simple man. What I have in my hand is an official paper signed by the provincial judge stating your boat will be seized by the authorities. Your boat is too old. It is no longer seaworthy. Furthermore, it states you are to be arrested promptly for fishing without a permit." Miss Kwai smiled smugly. "But most certainly this paper could easily be cast into the river and your boat will remain yours, and you will not be arrested should you agree to help your fellow countrymen through this major transition."

Gim Shay fumed with anger. "Go to hell! My life is what I make of it. The government cannot hand out happiness as a storekeeper would hand me a bag of rice."

The big-city woman responded with an admiring grin. She had gained a certain respect and fondness for the gritty, independent fisherman. "Ah, but Mr. Shay—you will be happy and content, the government so orders it. And did I mention your friend Fat Lee will also be arrested? And both your homes, I regret to mention, will be leveled."

Fat Lee's jaw dropped and his eyes widened with shock and fear. Gim Shay stood his ground. "No! And no again, if you did not understand my first reply. I would rather die in prison than force my fellow villagers to eat the human waste of the lies you wish me to feed them."

Suzie Kwai's face began to reflect a more serious and determined appearance. "Mr. Shay, it will be at least a year before the lake waters consume your home. Where will you and Mrs. Shay live should your lovely home be destroyed? The monkey caves that dot the gorge?"

"Loyal friend, you can't allow my family to starve in a bat-infested cave," said Fat Lee. "Please do as the woman asks. After all I've done for you, you cannot do this to me and my family."

"You're not a friend. You, like most other villagers, hurt me because I could not speak good when I was young. You are only my partner because your father loaned me the money long ago to buy my boat. I have already repaid you by allowing you to fish in my boat," Gim replied, rolling his eyes in contempt.

Embarrassed, the much taller Fat Lee turned his head away, not wanting his old companion to look him in the face. "I...I...we only wanted to make jokes, we did not think you were hurt by such harmless fun."

"Go to hell, Fat Lee. Forgive me—I have already asked you to make this journey before, but then you have never done as I have asked," quipped Gim.

Tears began to roll down the proud face of Fat Lee.

"It was my turn to hurt you," Gim chortled. "But I will not allow your children to live in a cave." He turned to Miss Kwai. "I will go with you to do this foolish thing."

"Excellent!" Miss Kwai said. "My fisherman friend, please get in my boat. Mr. Lee can take your boat back to the harbor for you. We have no time to waste. A car awaits you at the dock, and from there you will be driven to Chongqing and your destiny."

Reluctantly, the short, white-bearded fisherman boarded the speedboat. In less than an hour the high-powered boat ran up the murky Yangtze to the village dock. Gim eyed a gleaming, sleek, black *gwai lah* limousine pulling into the harbor.

He had ridden in an automobile only once before, when as a young man he rode in an ambulance to the village infirmary after breaking his leg falling off a rock and into the dangerous Yangtze. This was the longest car Gim had ever seen. The old fisherman couldn't help but chuckle under his breath, thinking how silly it was to have such a long and expensive automobile to carry a poor, uneducated villager.

Much of the entire village had gathered around the finely polished car to gawk at something few people from Qin Din had ever seen.

"The world waits for you, my instant celebrity," proclaimed Miss Kwai as she led Gim to the waiting limousine.

Speechless, the villagers watched with amazement as the man they had shunned and mocked as a child stepped into the gleaming vehicle. Feeling uncomfortable, Gim slipped into the cavernous Cadillac interior. To his chagrin, he saw Sin sprawled across the wide back seat, once again guzzling Double Happiness beer.

"Well, my handsome husband, I knew you would come to your senses eventually," she slurred with a grin.

"Curse you, my loving wife. You knew I could not bear to have my boat taken from me," Gim replied.

"Foolish man! Your boat will serve you no good purpose once they ship us off to the Gobi," giggled Sin.

Gritting his teeth in annoyance, Gim said, "I had planned on bringing my boat with me to the Gobi. I will find waters there to fish."

Sin began to cackle hilariously, spilling beer on her lap. "Slow, stupid man. What do you plan to fish for in the Gobi—scorpions? The Gobi is a dry, burned-over wasteland. I can piss you a larger river than any you would find there."

Embarrassed by his ignorance, Gim slumped down on the seat and covered his face with his hands despairingly. He dared not look up at his wife or the onlookers peering through the tinted glass.

As they left the small village, Gim sat up and stared in silence at the passing scenery. Miss Kwai spoke endlessly on her cell phone and his wife consumed more of the Double Happiness beer that was provided for their long ride to Chongqing. Gradually, the rural landscape transformed into a more urban setting.

"There must be nearly a hundred thousand people in Chongqing!" Gim exclaimed as he viewed the countless high buildings and increasing auto traffic.

Sin and Miss Kwai began to laugh heartily.

"Mr. Shay, you are indeed a village bumpkin. Chongqing has a population of perhaps 33 million. If it is not the world's largest city, it is certainly one of them," said Miss Kwai.

Gim had never seen so many people and such tall buildings. Already feeling uneasy being out of his element, he felt embarrassed after displaying his ignorance about the size of Chongqing.

The limousine crept slowly on the city streets, fighting the heavy pedestrian and vehicle traffic. After nearly two hours of moving at a snail's pace, the long car finally arrived at one of Chongqing's newly constructed high rises.

"Welcome, Mr. and Mrs. Shay, to China's brand new National Television Network building. Your fifteen minutes is about to begin," announced Miss Kwai.

"My what?" Gim asked.

"Never mind," replied Miss Kwai as a group of well-dressed people walked briskly toward them.

"Greetings," said a young woman who closely resembled Miss Kwai in both physical appearance and dress. "I am Yoon Fee. You may address me as J.J. I am here to look after you while you are here in Chongqing. I will make sure you are not abducted by aliens," she chuckled. "First we must prepare you for your television appearance. Mr. and Mrs. Shay, please come…"

Before the woman could complete her sentence, Sin, who was now quite intoxicated, dropped to the sidewalk and began throwing up in the gutter. Quickly, two aides assisted the oafish woman to her feet.

Miss Kwai giggled nervously. "Please excuse Mrs. Shay. The stress of her future fame is a heavy stone to carry. She is also car sick."

"Most certainly. Make this couple as presentable as possible. We begin shooting within the hour," ordered J.J. to her subordinates.

Gim and Sin were whisked into two separate dressing rooms. They were surrounded by myriad people, grooming and dressing them in various styles and colors, determining in which clothing they would look most suitable before the cameras. Both Gim and Sin were becoming overwhelmed as the attendants hovered over them like adoring drone bees attending to their queen.

"What are you doing?" cried Gim, sitting in a thickly padded chair.

"Applying makeup. You want to look beautiful for the camera, do you not?" responded an effeminate-looking man.

"Damn you sir—or is it miss?—I am a fisherman, not a Shanghai whore!" Gim exclaimed, slapping the man's hand away.

Despite his protests, Gim was transformed in to more of an idealized iconic image than that of a real man. The exaggerated makeup made him resemble more a Chinese opera singer than a fisherman. With his newly manicured fingernails and finely pressed lime-green silk Mao jacket, he bore little resemblance to a man who made a living from hard manual labor.

The nervous Gim was escorted into a large taping studio. An enormous movie screen covered one of the walls. Sin had already arrived in the studio. She was surrounded by makeup artists and wardrobe personnel, placing the finishing touches on her.

Gim's wife, like himself, had turned into someone very different.

"Wife, you look like a lady of the evening," chided Gim.

"Husband, you look like a clown," Sin fired back.

"Mr. and Mrs. Shay, you both look so divine!" Miss Kwai enthused.

"Splendid!" J.J. added. "The two of you look so natural for the parts you will play to encourage the gorge people to move."

Fronting the huge screen, a young man began arranging a stack of huge cue cards.

"We begin taping soon, my friends. The two of you are about to become immortal!" Miss Kwai exclaimed. "Every television, newspaper, and posters around the nation will have your faces on them."

"I thought immortal meant not dying?" asked a puzzled Gim.

"Never mind, just read the lines with your names next to them on the cue cards once the red light goes on," commanded Miss Kwai. "Understand?"

"Uh…no…" replied Gim as Sin shook her head with bewilderment.

"Good. We'll start immediately," Miss Kwai said, not waiting or caring for any reply from the couple.

Bright flood lights focused on the couple. The red light on the television camera lit up. The energetic reporter's mouth widened, revealing her perfectly straight, very white teeth.

"To the people of our great country, good evening. I am Suzie Kwai, chief roving reporter for the People's Republic Television Network. I have the distinctive pleasure of introducing to you Mr. and Mrs. Gim Shay. They are true patriots of China. They willingly and happily accept their relocation to the Gobi once the waters begin to rise behind the monumental Three Gorges Dam that will rocket our nation to the stars of glory."

Miss Kwai continued: "Insightful, loyal citizens like Mr. and Mrs. Shay not only agree with the relocation plan, they welcome it. They are elated to leave the Three Gorges for the double happiness that awaits them in the Gobi," she proclaimed with pompous rhetoric. "Mr. and Mrs. Shay, please tell the viewers in your own words the pride and joy you feel toward the Three Gorges Dam project and your joyous opportunity to begin a new life in the Gobi."

As Miss Kwai spoke, images of the Three Gorges Dam's construction were projected on the giant screen behind them.

Gim and Sin trembled with stage fright, unable to utter a single word.

"Damn it," Miss Kwai mouthed through a frozen smile. "Read the lines on the cards!"

"I...I...we..." stuttered Gim and his wife collectively.

"Crap. Stop the cameras!" shouted the exasperated newswoman. "My friends, relax. Just read the lines beside your names on those big cards." Miss Kwai was growing more and more annoyed. "Can't you two read?" she added rhetorically.

"No, I cannot read," Gim Shay replied. "My beautiful wife can read, but she is drunk."

"Shit! Then we'll dub in your voices," said Miss Kwai, rolling her eyes.

"What is dub?" asked Gim.

"It is not important. You and your wife simply move your lips when the young man over there with the cards points to you."

Throughout that day and the next two, they shot the propagandistic film over and over again. After much effort and tribulation, the footage was finally completed. But no sooner did it end when the beleaguered couple had yet another film to do before they could finally return to the gorge—the only home they had ever known.

Once more the pair stood awkwardly under the hot studio lights, again being meticulously preened by a host of wardrobe and makeup personnel—much like a grandmother doting over a favored grandchild.

"Kids, hold these bottles," said J.J. "Now, wait until I cue you—then drink them as if you've been stranded in the hot Gobi for a long time. Uh…stranded in the Sahara for a long time."

"What is this?" asked Gim.

"It is the *gwai lah* sweet drink Coca Cola," replied J.J.

Gim took a sip and quickly spit out the liquid. "It is so sweet! I would prefer the *lo fon* drink Pepsi that you provided for us in our hotel room," grumbled the fisherman.

"I too find the *gwai lah* drink too sweet," Sin added, her right eye twitching as usual. "Do you have any Double Happiness?"

"Damn this!" J.J. burst out. "Village fools! Idiots! Coca Cola is paying you a vast sum of money to endorse their product. It makes no difference that you like it or not. You need only to pretend to like it!" J.J. was now shouting. "Bring on the dancing girls! At least they will do as I say without question."

"Is this custom in eye fowl for people to say they like something which they do not?" questioned Gim naively.

"My dear villagers, we say things we do not believe in all the time. We tell people what they want to hear. It is not wrong per se, if it makes the people feel good," J.J. retorted.

Doing as they were told, the couple gulped the *gwai lah* soft drink with make-believe enthusiasm while dancing girls pranced about in the background to the beat of a Britney Spears song.

"Coca Cola! It is as refreshing as the morning mist off the Yangtze!" exclaimed Sin, wearing a ludicrous grin.

"Yes! As refreshing as a summer breeze," added Gim with an equally pretentious smile.

After two weeks of performing before cameras and glad-handing significant dignitaries and bureaucrats, it was finally time for the exhausted couple to return to their small village up river. Gim and Sin welcomed the return to normalcy in the gorge.

Already their endorsements of the Three Gorges relocation plan had begun airing on televisions across China, and their faces were plastered on posters and in newspapers across the nation.

"Snapping their fingers," mumbled Gim on their return trip to Qin Din.

"What did you say?" asked Miss Kwai.

"It is of no importance, Miss Kwai," Gim said tersely, reflecting on the shameful sight of the dancing girls snapping their fingers in the Coca Cola commercial.

During the long ride home, the young reporter placed her hand on Gim's knee and smiled warmly. "Mr. and Mrs. Shay, you have honored your nation very well. Many of your fellow countrymen will no longer fear leaving their former lives in the gorge to start an adventurous new life higher up the gorge wall or in the Gobi. You will both have an honored place at the ribbon-cutting ceremony atop the great gorge dam in a few months. The premier himself will present the two of you with an original piece of cement that was used in the making of the great dam." The entire time Miss Kwai spoke, her cell phone remained glued to her right ear.

Gradually, the limousine dropped down into the gorge on the snake-like, winding road. Gim noticed a large gathering in the village below. The old fisherman pointed the swelling crowd out to his wife. Both were puzzled by such a large gathering.

As they neared the village square, the immense throng of villagers began cheering the return of their native son and daughter.

"My beloved patriots, those little people of Qin Din have come to honor the both of you," Miss Kwai said. "Not since the Great Wall has our mother country built something so monumental as the Three Gorges Dam. You must take double pride that you are both a part of this wonderful project, so to speak."

The limousine came to a halt.

"Gim! Gim! Sin! Sin!" reverberated the collective cries of the zealous crowd.

Colored paper folded into crowns was placed atop the couple's heads.

"Welcome back to Qin Din. Here is your Moses and your Mrs. Moses!" proclaimed Miss Kwai to the adoring crowd.

Gim and Sin exited the limousine. The villagers lifted them onto their shoulders. Sin raised her arms high into the air, laughing hysterically, elated by the attention she had once relished when she was young and beautiful.

Gim felt quite uncomfortable by the praise and stares of the people who had ignored him for so long. He could do no better than wave feebly and attempt to force a smile.

The circus-like scene appeared even more exaggerated with the presence of blinding flashbulbs from the media, continually going off in their eyes.

"Gobi! Gobi! We will have double happiness in our new home," shouted a reveler.

Free beer, Coca Cola, and food were provided in the village square. For the remainder of the day and into the night the boisterous mob partied. Two lengths of gold-painted bamboo sticks, representing regal batons, were presented to Gim and Sin, and the couple was seated upon two chairs on a platform in the square. Little girls presented Sin bouquets of fresh flowers. Seated on their thrones, the couple appeared more clown-like in appearance than they did an actual royal couple.

"We love you both, our cherished friends," said Fat Lee and his wife while shoving bottles of Double Happiness beer into their hands.

It was near daylight when most of the merrymakers finally collapsed about the square after consuming excessive amounts of food and drink. In the light of day, Gim and Sin, still wearing their paper crowns, staggered to their ramshackle stone house overlooking the Yangtze.

Gim lit a lantern and they sat together on the bed holding

hands—something they had not done in a great while. Sin then closed her eyes and rested her head on Gim's shoulder—another small kindness Gim's wife had not demonstrated in recent history.

"My dear husband, I have been a disappointment to you, have I not? I was once beautiful. My stomach was flat and my eye did not twitch."

Gim laughed robustly in response. "My silly fat wife—I am but a poor fisherman of simple mind. I was never handsome at any age, and as a child I spoke with much difficulty. The villagers laughed at me as if I were a trained monkey doing tricks for peanuts." He began to chuckle more heartily. "Does it really matter if you disappoint such a fool?"

Sin began to laugh along with her husband. "How correct you are, my husband. You are a stupid, unattractive man. It is of no consequence that I have disappointed you all these years." She paused and adjusted the paper crown resting atop her head. "But at least we now have the respect of our fellow villagers."

Gim began to cackle as absurdly as his wife. "We do look so grand in our paper crowns, do we not?" Groggy from a night of heavy drinking, Gim strained to rise off the bed. Speaking nothing further, he walked out the front door.

"Where are you going, my husband?" asked Sin.

There was no response from the old fisherman as the door slowly closed behind him.

Gim walked to the river's edge. The choking, polluted air that often floated up from Chongqing made it difficult for him to breathe. He removed his paper crown and gazed at it as one would gaze at a found object, unsure of its purpose or meaning. He then flung it as hard as he could into the river. The bright, mauve-colored paper contrasted sharply with the dark-green water.

Gim watched his crown float far away, oblivious to the vociferous clinking, pounding, and pinging sounds that resonated from the dam construction site, just a few miles downstream. Gim chortled in a half-hearted way, thinking there had been so few moments in his life when he had felt any real joy. How important could his life have been if the only great day he had known was the recent day he had battled the enormous carp, only to lose it because of Miss Kwai?

My life is nothing, thought Gim. *I was a joke to everyone in Qin Din, and now I am a joke to all of China—maybe the world.*

He began to search the beach, inspecting the various sized rocks that were scattered about. "This one should do nicely," Gim said aloud, stooping to lift a large rock. "This heavy stone will grant me a swift escape from this horrible hell."

He grasped the smooth, river-washed stone and walked into the cold, opaque waters of the Yangtze. His weighted burden swiftly pulled him to the bottom of a deep hole he had often fished. Rolling and tumbling in the strong current, Gim was carried downstream. Nearing unconsciousness, his numb hands soon lost their grip on the large stone, and he floated back to the surface. Breaking the water in an explosion of spray, Gim gasped to inhale life-giving air.

His body ached as he pushed himself onto shore, though there was little feeling in his arms and legs. He scanned the riverbank. He had traveled a good distance from where he had entered the river. "So damn cold! I must die a better way," Gim proclaimed as he stumbled to his feet.

Coughing river water from his lungs, Gim wobbled his way back home. He opened the door casually, as if returning from a stroll.

Sin looked at her husband with equal dispassion. "Have you been swimming?" she asked.

"That I was, my dear wife," he replied.

"Life will not be so bad on the Gobi—you'll see," said Sin, drying her husband's hair with a towel.

"I will…we will grow the best radishes in the whole Gobi," the old fisherman said. "Life goes on, does it not?"

"I hope there will be Double Happiness beer there," Sin pondered as she pulled a beer from her jacket that she had pocketed from last night's celebration.

Together they walked to the beach below their house and sat side by side on the sand. They shared their favorite beverage and stared at the Yangtze one final time before they were shipped off to the Gobi—never again to return to the Three Gorges.

— The End —

About the Author

William Wong Foey holds multiple degrees in Fine Art and Social Studies. Mr. Foey taught high school art, and has won numerous awards for creative writing. He has had short stories published in the *Chico News & Review, San Francisco Magazine, Watershed Magazine,* and the *Trans-Pacific Periodical.*

Mr. Foey is of Chinese/American descent, and his family has resided in Red Bluff since the 1850s. He is a frequent speaker on the history of the Chinese in America, including interviews on TV and in periodicals. He is currently a freelance artist and writer.